SUPERB WRITING
TO FIRE THE IMAGINATION

I wrote *The Worm in the Well* as a school play some years ago, about the time of the middle crusade. I still keep seeing the little libbards who acted in it, now quite grown up, in the street, and the occasional cockatrice; and recently a basilisk – though that might have been my own reflection in a shop window.

Contents

1	The Greenwood and the Well Long Ago	1
2	The Trip to Jerusalem	24
3	Alan Goes Fishing About Now	46
4	Alan's Second Bidding at the Well	56
5	Alan in the Holy Land	70
6	The Worm in the Greenwood	82
7	The Worm in the Village	95
8	Margaret in the Greenwood	102
9	Alan Speaks with Granny Shaftoe Again	115
10	The Third Bidding	121
11	The Last Bidding	134

The Trip to Jerusalem

Hello,
I am the trip to Jerusalem.
   I wait here for people to ride me
all the way to Jerusalem,
   wherever that is.

I am the idea of where you want to go,
   always ready for the road,
to amble, or gallop, or trot
   I don't care which – I'll go.

I don't mind how I travel:
   it's always towards Jerusalem.
Shall we get there by candlelight?
   And back again? O pilgrim,

Jerusalem is where you want to be:
   where all the pilgrims go.
I am the skytrain waiting to take you
   on your trip to Jerusalem.

Climb on at any station;
   I go just as you like all the way
If you want to stopover you may –
   I'm used to folk taking a long time.

Now you think you've got there,
   get off and I'll go back for another
traveller – it's quite a trade.
   How do you mean, you might not like it here?

That's your affair, pilgrim;
   your charter brought you what you asked;
you don't get your money back:
   we trips to Jerusalem are all one-way.

I don't know why you wanted to come –
   perhaps you had the wrong idea,
being one of these modern tourists.
   But I am the old-fashioned trip to Jerusalem.

   Farewell.

ONE

The Greenwood and the Well
Long Ago

'But have I seen wisdom?' asked the witch, swinging the two boys round with bony hands to face her, their backs against the wooden wall of her hut, the deeply-grooved and unforgiving bark of a Great Ash Tree in the greenwood. 'Clever and canny you are; young and lithe I can see. But wise? Is that so?'

Robin felt his mouth open, like the village gobdrool's, but too dry to dribble. He was alarmed, but not to the point of desperation. 'We are going fishing,' he said, his tongue stiff as bread.

'Fishing,' said Meric beside him. He was terrified, and looked a hundred years old, all his bones showing up and down his face, one hand out between him and the woman. The other seemed to be holding his side. His hair stood up in fright.

'Fishing?' said the witch. 'What's your bait? Where's your water?'

'Saint Oswald's Well,' said Robin. 'Please.'

Little Margaret was not merely listening to this story. She was in it, living it, and not looking at what her embroidery needle was doing.

The needle bit her. Blood bubbled up on her thumb. Tears sprang from her eyes. She was only five.

Robin, describing an event of his childhood long ago, paused for a moment. Nurse came into the room and took Margaret away, calling her 'My little chitterling, my obsie-pobsie duckie,' and so on, remarks that made Robin grind his teeth.

'Did your naughty unkie frighten my little twinkle, then?' Nurse continued, smacking her lips reproachfully. Margaret yelled with terror at the sight.

The curtain closed behind them. They went down the spiral stair, out of hearing.

'Go on, Father,' said Alan. He had not been embroidering but filing the tip of a blunted arrow. He had cut himself once or twice, but he was older than his cousin Margaret and had not minded that or the tale of the witch.

'Another time,' said Robin. 'I must go and inspect the guard.'

When Robin and Meric had come into the clearing beside the Great Ash Tree the little hut had been there, with a goat tethered to a post eating the grass. Small smoke from a tiny fire had been rising from the roof, so that someone was inside.

'If it's our people,' Meric had said, 'I don't know why they're building in the greenwood.' Without any more sign he had strode across, pitched the door to one side and gone in.

He did not have to bend his head. Robin had gone in after him, and had to bend his. Meric was younger and smaller, but more bossy.

Something buzzed like bees against Robin's ear as he went in, and then the witch rounded on them both, and put them against the wall.

Outside, the bright leaves of the greenwood hung under a blue and white sky full of summer birds. A jay chattered across the clearing, doves clattered out of the branches, and rooks swirled in the air.

Robin saw another thing in the doorway. He had been seeing it for some time, but every time he understood it he no longer did. It had first been a cat. Then, on being understood as a cat, it stopped being cat, and began being almost anything else. Dog, for instance. It was dog when Robin knew it was, and then changed away towards owl.

For a comfortable moment it was a libbard. Meric's armorial bearings had a libbard in them, so this thing might have to do with him. The witch would then be incapable of harming Meric, and probably Robin himself too.

The books say a libbard is a leopard that is a lion that is walking across your vision passant-gardant, looking at you. The looking is not described, because no one has lived to tell.

The thing stopped being a libbard as soon as it was it, like all the dreams of life. A roe deer stood in the doorway for just as long as it could be understood. Antlers grew, and sprouted leaves. The thing was a man with that head, then a man with a wolf's head. In the middle of the greenwood that was the end of all hope.

No time had gone by. The witch was still speaking, still searching them with her eyes.

'Not many visit Granny Shaftoe,' she said. 'Not many come to fish Saint Oswald's Well.' She followed Robin's eyes to where they watched the thing in the doorway. 'Down, down, Thalumar,' she called. 'Down and rest. Stop teasing.'

The shape subsided almost to invisibility, but shimmered like the shadow of fire in sunlight.

Beyond, the greenwood lay quiet, as if it had stopped.

Meric, hissing a breath inwards, had begun to move suddenly. The hand at his side came out with a knife in it, and the knife diving for the witch. Breath came out of Meric's mouth in a screaming cry.

The witch fell back a pace, her eyes on the knife.

'I will kill you,' said Meric, in the middle of his shout, frightened to desperation.

What was in the doorway resolved into something darker than coiling shadow and became as black as the pit, and more huge. The pit is the everlasting darkness of Hell, which has been mentioned in books, but the drawings are inexact. This darkness expanded slow enough to be seen, too quickly to be avoided. It hit like thunder and overpowered like a flood. When it came over Robin there was nothing left of the world, and he was nothing in it.

That had been so many years ago. Robin, Lord of the Dale, told it again to Alan and Margaret, who was usually called Alan's cousin, because she was ladylike even if no one knew where she had come from.

'Go on, Father,' said Alan, another day, wintering by the fire, reminding Robin of where he had got to. Nurse was well out of hearing in the kitchens.

'I thought I would not live,' said Robin. 'And that Meric . . . Oh, Meric, what became of you?'

'What did?' asked Alan. 'Who is Meric?'

'Lord of Eastmarch, beyond the forest,' said his father. 'He got his own way every time, and never thought there could be any other way. But he was my friend, and we had gone fishing together that day.'

'And what did you catch?' asked Alan, even though he knew he should not ask.

'I will go to my embroidery,' said Margaret, knowing the same thing, very worried at the way the Lord of the Dale was looking, recalling that she did not like this tale at all. 'An it please you, my eame.' That is how you speak to noble uncles.

'Aye,' said Robin. And when she had curtseyed and gone he looked at Alan, and said, 'It is time to tell you more. And we were but boys.'

Robin was lying in the grass of a forest clearing, and all round him the trees were recovering from the impact of a great gust of wind. The undersides of leaves showed, the branches still heaved, and the crowns still swayed. Birds were tumbling down the sky, and clouds rising and dancing against the blue.

There was no hut. There was no witch. Meric lay

face down, his right arm stretched out, and its hand holding something no longer there, so tightly that the flesh of his hand was pulled back and whitened.

In the instant that he woke the hand relaxed. He flexed it and looked at it, and then all round him.

'Can't sit here all morning,' he said, shaking his head to clear it. 'Saint Oswald's Well is yonder. My father says the eels sleep there, and he has caught swallows in winter.' He stood up and walked on, nothing in his mind but the fishing. 'I wish we had a fire to cook the fish on. We have a man who doesn't do anything but light fires for us.'

He was Meric again, with something lost from his memory. Robin knew he had forgotten the hut.

'This way,' said Meric, knowing he was right without knowing why. He knew where the well had to be, without ever being there.

Robin followed him, remembering a witch, the thing in the doorway, and that Meric had drawn a knife.

That was Meric, who had everything because his father had more land and more people. The Lords of Eastmarch had been given more than the Lords of the Dale, and that was all right until Meric talked about it without having to try.

It gave him more authority, too. He was the leader

because of being born Meric. But being first in everything did not make him the wisest in any.

'He was that sort of boy,' said Robin. 'People like you and me do what happens to us. Meric would make them happen, even if that killed him in the process. Have you a friend like that, that you would die for? And wouldn't care if he had caused your death?'

'I do not know anyone,' said Alan. 'Margaret is only a girl.'

Meric's mind was empty of remembrance of the hut — and he was not the guilt-feeling sort.

'I shall catch the biggest ones,' he said, was saying, had been washing Robin's mind with the thought all the way. 'You fish that side, and I shall fish this.' He was talking quickly, giving firm orders, unable to imagine they could be disobeyed by Robin, destiny, or anything.

'You will use a midden-worm, Robin,' he decided. 'I shall use a coney's tongue. It has been in moonlight for three nights and stinks rotten. I have mealworms too, which have eaten only wheat, not barley or oats or rye. Warm them for me under your tongue. Your midden-worms are happy cold.'

Saint Oswald's Well was the source of a little brook. Water bubbled and rippled into a pool from a mound of boulders. Low shelves of stone made the banks, and the water ran out at the far end over another. The waters of the pool went down clear into deep darkness.

Beside the water Meric went on talking. Words and commands bubbled from him, faster and faster while he still expected to catch the first fish.

There was a gap, strong with silence, when Robin's line tightened, he lifted out a gasping fish, and laid it on the bank his side.

'You were very lucky,' said Meric, quite deeply offended by what had happened, 'but fish cannot resist coney's tongue three nights under the moon.'

In spite of that, Robin caught four fish. He laid them one by one on the flat stone, where they lifted their tails, drank air, and died. There were longer silences from Meric's empty bank at each catch. The coney's tongue had not charmed any fish to his hook.

'My fish will be bigger than them,' said Meric. 'Your people have been poaching on my side of the water. That is the reason. Is it not the reason?'

'I think it is bad luck,' said Robin. He caught a fifth fish and threw it back to grow larger.

'We do not have that,' said Meric. To have Robin

throw fish back angered him. 'It is quite wrong.' He considered other ways of taking fish home.

'We came together, to share the fishing,' he said at last. 'Of course I would have shared with you, so you will share with me.'

'I shall keep these,' said Robin. 'But I will catch some for you now. I am being lucky.'

'But I wish to go home,' said Meric. 'I shall have the keeper whipped because he has cheated me. These are not coneys' tongues, but weasels' or other vermin. We shall share the fish we have now. That is fair.'

'I will give you one of these,' said Robin. 'And the next one I catch. That will be fair.'

But Meric was tired of fishing. Or perhaps he had remembered a little of what had happened before they got here and was no longer comfortable in the forest. 'You will have three, and I will have two,' he said. 'I want three more than you want three.'

'I will catch one more again,' said Robin. 'That will be three each.'

'You are not listening,' said Meric. 'I will not take the biggest ones. Just one big one and two small ones. One day I shall be a greater lord than you, because the Lords of Eastmarch have more land.'

He was beside Robin now, on that side of the pool, fingering the silvery fish, wanting them so much.

'Leave them,' said Robin, winding in his line. 'They are mine, Meric.'

'I will leave the biggest,' said Meric. 'I shall say we both caught them and three are my share.'

'You must speak the truth,' said Robin. 'The truth is that you have caught none. The truth is that you are no good at fishing. The truth is that you do not know how. The truth is that I shall take all these fish home with me.'

'The truth is what happens,' said Meric, taking up one fish and then a second, and feeling for his knife. 'I shall put them on a string,' he said.

'I shall have to fight you,' said Robin.

'When I win I shall take the largest fish,' said Meric, still feeling for his knife.

'I am bigger than you,' said Robin. 'How can I fight you fair?'

'I shall take all the fish,' said Meric. 'I shall have won them. You are making it easy for me.'

'You must put your knife down,' said Robin, remembering Granny Shaftoe.

'I can't find it,' said Meric, discovering its sheath empty, and looking round. 'I had it when I set off this morning. Did you see me drop it?'

'No,' said Robin. 'I did not see you drop it.'

'We will fight three shoulder-falls,' said Meric; and

before he had finished making the arrangements he leapt forward, tipped Robin over, and had him on his back. 'One to me,' he said, helping Robin up, then, before Robin was fully on his feet again, doing the same trick. 'Two,' he said. The truth is that you have lost twice. The truth is that you are no good at fighting. The truth is that you do not know how. The truth is that I shall take all these fish home with me.'

Robin had bitten his tongue. Tears had come to his eyes. His elbows hurt. He was becoming angry, like a small monster. He was not like the owl or the libbard, because he was extremely real and not merely teasing in a doorway. Robin stayed on the ground and worked out how to deal with the problem.

If Meric could see me truly, he thought, he would understand that I am changing from one thing to another, from cat to dog, from dog to libbard, from libbard to wolf, and so on.

'I think I won,' said Meric, and bent to look at the fish again.

Robin got to his feet slowly. He wanted to be up and in charge before the next part of the fight began.

'Well,' said Meric, looking over his shoulder at him, not troubling to turn to face him.

It was easy for Robin to knock him into Saint

Oswald's Well, and satisfying too, but not the end.

Meric went under and scrambled to his feet. The water seemed not deeper than his knees, so that he could put his arms on the stone ledge that ran round the pool. He blew water out of his mouth.

'We shall go on until you give in,' said Robin.

'Winner takes all,' said Meric.

'You are having none of my fish,' said Robin.

Meric grabbed his ankle and dragged him into the water.

When they were both in neither could stand up without falling over, and no one could possibly fight. The quarrel seemed strange and ridiculous, but unfortunately it was about four fish and their ownership, which could not be settled without the fight. So that had to go on, or begin; but had to come to an end.

They agreed that Robin should climb out on his side of the water, Meric on his, and meet again in the clearing, and the fight would go on until one of them gave up. Then they would share the fish two and two like Christians, wash their blood off in the well, and go to one house or the other for the night and eat the fish. They argued it out standing in the water, shouting as loud as they could, each regretting anything he had to agree to, but sticking to their words by swearing it on

13

their lords' honour (which was their fathers', in either case).

They were climbing out of the water when the sky grew dark and a shadow fell across the grass. It was not a matter of clouds, or of anything in the sky, but something in the clearing itself, as if it filled with invisible but dense smoke, so that seeing became difficult.

Something came through the thick twilight, something indistinct but that had its own shape, long and low and many-legged; something that also wanted to appear as other things. To Robin it now appeared as a loping pack of wolves, then as rolling boulders, and again as a troop of soldiers hastening on a dark mission. Always the appearance carried a dreadful sense of terror. It shifted its shape like the libbard, and this was not teasing but true horror; not something trifling and unmentionable like a libbard, or Hell, but something about the whole world; the whole world inside out.

It was something, it seemed to Robin, that you could not think of at all and stay sane.

It passed the length of Saint Oswald's Well, some few feet from Meric and from Robin. It ran, or rolled, or cantered, or glided, across the rest of the clearing, and went into the trees beyond. After it the cloudless

14

dark withdrew, leaving hollow sunshine of the end of a strange day.

'Did you see them?' asked Meric.

'Yes,' said Robin. 'Shall we go home now?'

'It is the first time I have seen the fairies,' said Meric. 'They were so beautiful I wanted to keep them. Shall we follow them?'

'They were as dreadful as the witch,' said Robin. 'Or the witch's animals.'

'I only saw fairies,' said Meric. 'Let's follow them. You bring the fish. You didn't see anything so you're jealous. You know they were beautiful.'

'I didn't see them,' said Robin. 'I didn't.'

'You are just being stupid,' Meric bellowed. 'Get the fish. You caught them; you carry them.'

But, although neither of them had ever taken their eyes away from the fish, there was nothing left. They had gone, leaving not a scale behind.

'The witch took them,' said Robin. 'I was watching them, and you didn't steal them . . .'

'Steal?' shouted Meric. 'Steal my own fish?'

'. . . and then I couldn't see them. Witches do that, you know.'

The sun had gone below the highest leaves now. The day was over. Both boys walked wet towards the road, where the drive cut through the greenwood.

'What witch?' said Meric, crossly. 'I don't know any witch?'

'This morning,' said Robin. 'We were in her hut.'

Meric shook his head. Water splashed from his wet long hair. 'I wouldn't go into a witch's hut.'

'You didn't know it was one,' said Robin.

'Of course I would,' said Meric. They plodded on under the trees, quite uncomfortable with wet. 'I dreamed about one once,' said Meric. 'I killed her with my knife. You just stood there like a girl.'

That was meant to be fighting talk, and usually was. But the time for that was over now. They walked on again, longing for road and fireside.

I wonder if he did, after all, thought Robin. She wasn't there any more.

'I would,' said Meric. 'If I hadn't lost it.'

In the forest behind them the owls began to move.

'And,' said Meric, 'it is lucky to see fairies.'

'Unlucky,' said Robin. 'Ask anybody.'

'The first person I meet,' said Meric. 'I will.'

So they went to their homes, home, wet to the crowns of their heads, without any fish at all.

'Now who's a crosspatch then?' said Robin's Nurse, the same one who was to be Alan's Nurse later, and Margaret's. 'Nursey doesn't mind if her little manny hasn't brought her a fishy, so there's no need to sulk,

Robbity-bobbity.' She took away wet clothes, talking to herself like a nutmeg grater.

And to think, Robin reflected, that Meric saw fairies, and I have that Nurse. He sat, wet and naked, on a stone step, and hated her.

'I can't see you,' said Nurse. 'Don't do those rude things, Master Robin. Heaven can see you even if I can't.'

It was very dispiriting to Robin, who had done nothing, only thought about it.

'Our same Nurse?' said Alan, when his father had finished. 'Or are they all exactly the same? Ours would say that. There couldn't be two of her.'

'The same Nurse,' said his father. 'She would have gone long since, but I couldn't raise you after your mother was no more. And that day it was better to be with her than to be in the forest. At least she was always doing her best, no matter how awful, which was better than Meric, who always did his worst, no matter how good.'

'And is Granny Shaftoe,' asked Alan, 'the Granny Shaftoe we all know, mad and wild and in the woods?'

'Mad and wise,' said his father. 'Servants say. Remember, she cured your wart.'

'She cured my wart,' said Alan. 'But go on.'

'Another day,' said his father. 'I must go and collect taxes, you know, heriots and blood money and amercements and dues and forfeits and distraints and copyholds. And don't I hear Nurse calling for you to go for lessons with Sir Ailred?'

There were other days, indeed. For many years Alan was not always sure whether what he was told had happened to him or to his father. Only when Meric came into the tale was he nearly sure his father had been the one in this other story.

Or there was always the possibility that Meric was a way his father had of looking at himself, his duplicate, the naughty one, who had broken a window (in the days when glass was almost a magic substance) or not wiped his feet (in the days when mud was the best thing you walked on outdoors).

Granny Shaftoe was always about in the centuries either side of that millennium. She pitched her little hut here and there in the greenwood, perched under a Great Ash Tree, or sheltered under a rock, and scratched a simple garden round it.

Servants from the castle, lasses from the village, lads hopelessly in love, or hopelessly out of love, went to Granny Shaftoe for charms. She was summoned to kill pigs for salting down. Robin's Nurse went to her to have her face turned green. At least, Robin assumed she had meant it to happen, he told Alan, discussing Granny Shaftoe one day, telling more stories about his times with Meric.

Meric did not see fairies again, and Robin was spared the things he had himself seen moving and roiling across the clearing. But his Nurse was always there, a sort of inquisitive goblin, enquiring impolitely about his insides, making him leave his best bits of dinner for Sir Manners, calling him her Coochie-Coochie Coo, running after him (like a moving bush) with a coat if he went outside on a fine and warm but merely rainy day.

'Just the same these days,' said Alan.

'They train them thoroughly,' said Robin.

When Meric's father died in a battle, where he had been speaking French and fighting Frenchmen for the King of England (who was also the King of France) Meric became Lord of Eastmarch. He was liable for service to the King, but luckily the King was now the French King (who was also King of England) but speaking English and fighting Englishmen, far off in Touraine. When these two Kings found they were one person it seemed pointless to carry on fighting, so they declared peace on each other. The knights went on fighting because that was their duty, but the King always said it was the other King who would pay them, so nobody did.

'I'm not going,' Meric had said, meeting Robin near a certain black hut, being watched by a certain witch and having her familiar spirit going through its range of shape-changes. Meric looked slightly away from all that disturbance to the view. 'We'll go fishing in Scotland,' he said. 'And knock a few Picts on the head. Shall we?'

'I'm busy this year,' said Robin. 'Sorry.'

'Actually getting married to your mother,' Robin told Alan, when he was around as a result. 'Or proposing to her several times a day.' Sometimes personally, sometimes by carrier pigeon.

'I think I'll go home,' said Meric, that day in the greenwood. 'What did you say you were doing, Robin?'

Robin was getting married to a nice girl from a romantic castle on a cliff-top. She was to bring him land, he said, when he got her to accept him.

'Land,' said Meric, looking round at the greenwood. 'It just gets people in it, and, well, other things. Anything else?'

'She loves me,' said Robin. 'That's all.'

Meric was instantly angry when someone he had

never met loved someone he knew, and hadn't considered his feelings at all. 'She won't be anybody much, I dare say.'

'Eleanor is her name,' said Robin.

'Oh well,' said Meric, getting over his rage, 'we'll have a big party the night before.'

Getting married, Robin thought, would be his best opportunity for getting rid of Nurse.

'You do it,' he said to Eleanor, when Sir Ailred, the priest, had splashed them with Latin words and rich holy smoke and they were home at the castle.

'She's so quaint,' said Eleanor. 'We might need it, so best keep it.'

So Robin still had Nurse (and so had Alan years later), smirking and using nicknames on him and fancying herself better than the other servants. At the feast she fell asleep under the table until next morning, then groaned and stood up, knocking herself out on the underside of the table. She staggered out on all fours and went to look for Granny Shaftoe and something for her headache.

Meric was at the feast too. He had become furious again about the wedding. 'You should have waited and let me get married first,' he said. 'You are only the son of a Lord, and I am an actual Lord. Besides, I would have chosen someone even prettier.'

But he stayed about a week, thinking things over, and went off to find a bride who would make Robin jealous – someone who was already a princess, perhaps, or who would later become a saint.

'She is bound to love me,' he said.

He found someone who perfectly understood him, did as she was told, and had her own way all the time. He liked her, and it made him nicer. He was supportive when Robin's father died out hunting, sent round a cook to help with the funeral tea, and came to check his dishes and the wine.

A year later came a message from the Pope and the king. Sir Ailred read it out in church in Latin, so no one understood it – you don't want anybody who is only nobody hearing important stuff.

Afterwards he explained it to the local Lords in English, or Anglo-Saxon, or Norman French, or even, for some of the older ones, Viking.

'Ah,' said Robin, hearing the English. 'At last.'

'Bingo,' said Meric.

'This is an emergency,' said Nurse, riving up good linen sheets like a professional ripster. 'They'll need bandages. I've seen it all before; there'll be nasty cuts; and tears before bedtime and they'll all say sorry and not mean it a bit.'

The message was for knights to join a Crusade to capture Jerusalem from the paynims, who had lived there a thousand years too long. The Pope had noticed it while revising the calendar. It should have been done in 4 AD, but paynims did not understand AD, using only heathen time as they did.

TWO

This is what Robin told Alan, bit by bit, long afterwards, getting the name wrong, in fact, because it was not

The Trip to Jerusalem

but the road back *from* Jerusalem.

The sun seemed never to fade from the beginning of the day until the end of it, Robin said. Then it would set and leave darkness that was hotter yet, taking the air with it.

The only water to be seen was unreal, lying in imaginary pools on actual ground. Sometimes there was rippling water, and then Robin, Lord of the Dale, would recall strange appearances in doorways in a far-distant English forest, long, long ago. Sometimes there were cities to be seen; once even Jerusalem itself.

'We shall never get there,' Meric, Lord of Eastmarch, said. 'This horse will die without a drink.'

Meric cared more for his horse than for his friends.

'So shall we,' said Robin.

They were in a rocky shelter under the rump of a ragged hill, somewhere in Syria, on the second day of being alone. They were sorry about it, and nothing they had brought seemed able to help them.

They had left the ranks of Crusaders together when some creatures like goats had showed themselves. At that time the long line of knights and baggage animals had been winding through a straggly woodland hardly the height of a man.

'Those are only goats,' Meric had said. 'We can run them down and then eat them.'

The goats were the fastest animals either of them had chased. What was more, they knew the country, had a clear sense of where to go, and were last seen high up an unclimbable cliff.

Robin and Meric were at the bottom of it, their helmets burning their heads, and their cuff links (of chain-mail) scorching their wrists.

Far above them carrion birds rose disturbed. An occasional dry pebble rattled its way down the red rocks from under the feet of the climbing goats. The goats were not hurrying any more. They had got to safety, and were doing a lot of passant-regardant stuff, which means walking across your vision while looking at you, like a lot of wildlife in those days.

Libbards do that. There were libbards in Syria, and two of them had eaten part of a boy two days before. Now they would eat two knights, Robin thought, wiping sweat from his face.

The goats went out of sight.

The sun, which had been shared by all the company of knights and men, suddenly shone on two of them alone. The cliff itself was hot as a bakestone.

It was bloody hot, Robin told Alan, those many years later. 'You'd get cockroaches in your greaves.'

'My eame,' said Margaret, 'you used an oath; and is greaves a proper word for me to hear?'

'Armoured trousers,' said Robin. 'But only below the knee, I assure you.'

'I will believe it,' said Margaret, primly.

When Robin and Meric had looked back the way they had come there was not a tree in sight. The low shrubs had vanished too. The ground they had covered looked merely like the bare cliff itself, laid on its side. Not very far away the world ended in a baffled haze, without a clear edge.

A lofty goat laughed invisibly, and some observant

vulture rang a mocking bell.

'We shouldn't have come,' Meric said. 'If you hadn't I wouldn't, so lead us back, Robin.'

'If I've got something, he shares it, thought Robin. And if he hasn't got anything I can share that. 'Have you any water?' he asked.

'Good idea,' said Meric, reaching for his leather bottle with the wooden ends.

'Don't drink,' said Robin. 'How are you going to fill it again?'

'There'll be a well,' said Meric. But as he said it he knew there would not be a well.

They looked at each other and both thought of that fight years ago in the greenwood, in and out of the water. Meric licked his gummy lips.

Robin thought of silvery fish laid on a stone.

'If the paynims capture us we shall be killed,' he said. 'It's them or the libbards.'

'Eh?' said Meric, looking at his helmet, which had a pair of dusty corduroy libbards on its top.

'Paynims,' said Robin, 'are much more likely.'

'We could take a sip,' said Meric. 'How much have you got?'

Robin's water bottle was nearly full. Meric's was all but empty. The contents had leaked out of the top and down Meric's throat.

'We'll share,' said Robin. He always said that.

'Share it out now,' said Meric. So they had shared the water out, half each.

In the close darkness the stars burnt hot. Where the ground began they stopped, and a pure blackness set in, empty and hostile.

Meric took off his sword and his sword belt and laid them on a rock he would be able to find easily. He did not find them again because every rock in Syria was exactly like that one.

Towards the third night Robin shared out his water again. They had both stopped pointing out the pools and lakes that covered the ground and were not there. They had given up the domes of Jerusalem every time they appeared. They had even abandoned faith in mountains that came now and then ahead of them. And the Crusade had always been some other person's idea.

They saw nothing living but themselves and the horses, except creatures from under rocks, certainly cockatrices, possibly basilisks. One would kill you if you touched it, the other if it saw you.

'Cor,' said Margaret.

'Now who's using an oath?' said Alan.

Robin thought that if he saw the basilisk, then he

would greedily look, without telling Meric. Meric could then make his own choices about lingering on in the dry dreadful desert.

On that third night there were sounds in that desert. There was the protesting voice of a camel, the rapid chatter of paynim voices. Later there was a single star of fire far below the rim of heaven.

'Can you fight?' said Robin. 'There are paynims yonder.'

'The truth is that I am no good at fighting,' said Meric. 'The truth is that I do not know how. The truth is that thirst or the paynims will kill me. In any case, you put my sword somewhere the other night and I have lost it. You should have remembered where it is. I thought that without water I would dry out like wood, and swell again when I drank. I did not know I should feel so ill and weak. I did not think I could be so unhappy. I shall try to fight. But what is there in the dark?'

'I do not know,' said Robin. 'But we took a vow to take Jerusalem or die in the attempt, and being lost here is not the attempt. We must attempt.'

'Why,' said Meric, 'did we quarrel about fish?'

'Because one of us is you,' said Robin.

'But the other is you,' said Meric. 'You don't quarrel, Robin, so it must be your fault.'

Meric's horse smelt water nearby and set off to find

it. Robin smelt the fire he could see, which was where the horse wanted to go too. So there was no more argument from Meric. He had to come too, because the horse that held him went to the water.

They made a nervous journey in the dark, creeping and stumbling, falling into the country's dry ditches, losing sight of the fire, losing the sense of the stars, until they were at the little hearth among the stones. A little glow simmered here, and up came smoke into eyes.

The horses were led away. The Lord of the Dale and the Lord of Eastmarch were so used to having horses led away that that did not alarm them.

'Like Nurse taking over,' said Robin. 'You can be ill just to please her. Meric was glad, too.'

'Those were paynims,' said Meric. 'Not our lads.'

It was too late for speech. The dark was dark enough, and arms that came out of it and held them. There is no fighting an enemy quite invisible. The only blow that Meric landed caught Robin on the ear. It was Robin who said he was sorry.

'That's all right,' said Meric.

They were both tied up in the dark much too near a camel. The horses went away happily towards water. They are captives anyway.

Four cups of water and two days later Robin and Meric were bought back by the King's treasurer for a fixed amount, about seven years' income. The King would be repaid when they returned to England, and that was that. It was all a cheat. The paynims got half the money, and the King kept the rest.

'I'm worth more than that,' said Meric.

'I'm glad I'm not,' said Robin.

'We shall have to get some booty from Jerusalem,' said Meric. 'Let's share the booty you get, Robin.'

A week later, once more journeying south to the Holy Land, they met the King of France returning. Jerusalem was still in the hands of the paynims, but the crusade was over for the time being and everyone was to return home. It was all another cheat.

The King of France took all the horses and went on his way. The English Lords were angry with their King for arranging things that way. They walked home. The King had managed to keep his horse. It was all explained by having separate kings for France and England these days, not just the same one changing sides. The King of Jerusalem was unhappiest, however, because it was thought he should pay all the costs. He had not been to Jerusalem either, and had only taken the job on because of the long holidays.

The walk home took thirteen weeks, all winter.

Towards the end the beggars of Flanders were throwing bones to English knights. Armour had all grown rusty, and the edges of swords been eaten away.

The last snow was dingy on the ground when Robin and Meric reached England, still there when they reached the court, and when they left it to go home.

'But in this land they understand our speech,' said Meric, more cheerful and calling for meat.

Robin was living on bread and cheese, which was cheaper. He had spent his money on sending a messenger ahead of them to say he was on his way. Meric had shared the messenger but not the cost.

'If he's going there he will pass by my castle,' he said. 'Milady will give him something to eat. That's all he'll want.'

If Meric does not eat he cannot walk, thought Robin, looking at him. I must wait for him.

They waited, and they travelled a little, and time passed so that Robin was greeted by the messenger he had sent ahead, meeting him on a great river bridge.

'Your lady sent me in turn with a message to you, my lord,' said the messenger, 'of her love and faith, wishing you to hasten to see your young son.'

'You have my thanks,' said Robin. 'And my lord of Eastmarch? Have you messages for him?'

'I must hurry on my way now, with no more to tell,' said the man, and off he went. Milady of Eastmarch had treated him badly, Robin thought, and not paid him to bring a message, so he had not done so. Robin had no money to buy it with, and it left with the man, and that was that.

Leaves were coming on the trees before the road ran again through familiar lands of the greenwood between the Dale and Eastmarch. There was a bright wind whipping up in the dusk where the road divided, one way to Eastmarch, the other to the Dale.

'They have put a post here,' said Meric, seeing a black stump standing in the grass. 'No, it is some one of my people, or yours, coming out to greet us.'

'Now my lords,' said the figure in black. Something beside her twinkled in the grass like a mirage, an imaginary waterfall in a thirsty mind.

'Now, old woman,' said Meric.

'Granny Shaftoe again,' said Margaret. 'She does live a long time, and know an awful lot.'

'There are limits,' said Robin. 'And we do not wish to know what she knows.'

'No, my eame,' said Margaret, quickly agreeing.

'It is Granny Shaftoe,' said Robin. 'Do you remember

that day we went fishing, Meric?'

'There was this old witch,' said Meric. 'I remember her. There was fishing. But not the two together, not on the same day. I could not catch a bite with her at hand.'

'You did not, my lord of Eastmarch,' said Granny Shaftoe. 'I warn you to stay away from that place. You woke something there, and it waits for you.'

'I have been to Jerusalem,' said Meric. 'Very nearly all the way. I cannot be harmed.'

'You can be warned,' said Granny Shaftoe, 'now that you are very nearly all the way back. I shall tell you, and what I say remember. Did you find wisdom in Jerusalem?'

'I shall next time,' said Meric. 'It was the French King's fault. Now stand aside, old woman.'

'Do not go to Saint Oswald's Well,' said Granny Shaftoe. 'Some thing waits there. Do not go.'

All at once she was there no longer, swallowed by the oncoming dusk, or the rising wind. Meric grinned in his usual way to show that nothing had happened at all.

'I'll be going on now,' he said, indicating the left hand road. 'It was a good Crusade,' he added, obviously remembering nothing about it.

Then he shook Robin's hand.

'We'll hunt soon,' he said. 'There'll be pig worth having still this month.'

'Pig,' said Robin, and watched Meric walk up the ride and among the young oaks at the greenwood edge.

Meric told his own family later what happened to him next. Robin could not say anything about it because he did not know. 'If I had known,' he would say, 'I could have done something about it sooner.'

The story went on here, to Meric alone, and this is what it was.

Meric followed the ride towards Eastmarch, under his own forest of oak, ash and beech, on his own land, a mile or two from home. In it ran his own deer, his own wild pig, his own wolves. He had been longing for return, but now he felt uneasy and unhappy, as if he could not welcome himself. No one had come to welcome him, not a peasant, not a hind, not a child, not a beggar. Even the bright wind that had been whipping up now lurked moodily among the trees.

It is that old woman, he thought. I shall see her off my land. She will have to go. I will not have nonsense where I live.

The wind suddenly flapped his cloak about him and whistled among the young leaves. The trees scraped at the greying sky. Then it dropped again, leaving a feeling of dread so strong it must be true.

Meric stood still and gathered his thoughts. I shall not be beaten, he decided. He lifted his head, looked about him at his own country, and walked on. He began to remember the way to places he had not seen for many years. This, on the right, was the clearing that held Saint Oswald's Well.

'And no old witch,' he said. 'Never.'

He left the road and followed a path into the clearing. Something stirred in his memory, more important than going straight home. Or not so much more important, but as if home did not exist.

The last of the light was resting on the well, a shaft of it piercing the clear quick water to its perpetual deep darkness. He stood for a while. On these stones had lain those fish, he thought, and could almost see them again.

Something touched the backs of his legs, pushing his cloak against him. A thrill like a thread of clear cold steel ran up his back and spread down his arms. His ears heard a sigh round them, his eyes saw the dusk turning solid beside the water, and something slid softly into the water with the smoothest ripple, down into the depths.

The light left the water and Meric was alone, or more than alone, standing empty of himself in the first folds of darkness.

She told me, he remembered. She told me not to

come. I have, and it cannot be undone.

'I told you not to come,' said a voice from beyond the water. 'You would not hear.' Granny Shaftoe stood yonder, a small beast beside her. Even in the dark it was darker, yet brighter, and a contrast.

'I did not understand,' said Meric. It was the first time he had ever admitted such a thing.

'All can be well,' said Granny Shaftoe. 'If you will do as I say now.'

'I will,' said Meric. 'What touched me?'

'I only know what may be,' said Granny Shaftoe, 'or what may not. Maybe you will remedy this.'

'I shall,' said Meric. 'I see you know.'

'When you go home,' said Granny Shaftoe, 'whatever greets you first, of any sort, you will take up in your arms and bring at once to this pool, Saint Oswald's Well, and throw it in. What lives here needs that. You yourself need that.'

'I shall do that,' said Meric. 'Have no fear.'

'I have none,' said Granny Shaftoe. 'Fear is yours. Go then, and make your choice.' Then she and her familiar beast were part of darkness again.

Meric went through the night to his castle. The moon came up and let him see his way. At the castle there was a great darkness and silence.

He came to the door alone, and opened the small

postern. There was light beyond, but no one stirred or came to greet him. No watch was kept, no sentry asked who he was.

The witch has twisted words, he thought. He stumbled against a stool, and woke something that trotted across the floor towards him, with light shining in its hair, and lifted its arms to him.

He picked it up, not sure what dog or bird it might be. It spoke to him, but he did not know what it said. Then light was being set on candles, people were coming forward, and he was known, but with a sort of frightened dread.

'What is it?' he asked. 'Do you not know me then, as I know you, John, Audrey? And where is milady?'

'My lord, come at once,' they said. 'Before it is too late.'

It was too late. When he took his wife's hand the warmth was running out of it, her eyes had closed; her last breath trembled on her lips with his name. And that was all.

From her wasted finger he drew the ring he had married her with.

'Too late,' he said.

'My lord,' said John, and Audrey curtseyed.

'And what is this?' asked Meric, holding up the child in his arms.

'That is your little Margaret,' said John.

'Poor soul,' said Audrey. 'She lost her mother. But she knew her father, and ran to you so pretty.'

'She ran to me so pretty,' said Meric. 'She greeted me the first of all. Be off with you, people. I shall be alone.'

They went. The little girl talked to him her baby talk, and then fell asleep. Meric gazed stunned at all that was around him, his wife dead on the bed, the child who had greeted him in his arms. And he recalled the words of Granny Shaftoe.

Whatever greets you first, of any sort, you will take up in your arms and bring at once to this pool, Saint Oswald's Well, and throw it in. What lives here needs that. You yourself need that.

Meric tried to slip the small gold ring on his little finger, but it would not go.

'I forgot her hand was so small,' he said.

'So small,' said the baby.

When he looked he saw his hands changing: where his fingers had been now grew curved claws, black and twisted. He considered the matter, and knew what he must do, and that there was no help for it.

He pulled a quilt from the bed, wrapped the sleeping baby, and went out into the night with her.

Leaves sprang out on the trees, oak, ash, beech. Winds of summer warmed them, guests of autumn darkened them, and they fell under winter. Clearings of the greenwood rattled and sang with them and frost sugared them. The dark depths of Saint Oswald's Well were tinctured and grew darker still.

Before the leaves came again the Lord of the Dale, Robin, lost his Eleanor. The sunshine of spring came to mock him, and the flowers of summer bloomed for others, not for him. It was not long ago in his stories, and he was never able to speak about it to Alan; but Margaret, sweet Margaret, was able to understand. It was to her he explained that he had called Meric, Lord of Eastmarch to the funeral, as he had called him to the wedding. But no answer had come from that castle.

'Doom has come upon me,' said Robin. 'What is there left?'

'There's a dumpsie-dearie then,' said Nurse. 'I mean you, Master Robin. I know, I'll bring in his own dearie-dumpsie. You'll both like that.'

'It smells,' said Robin. 'I don't care who it is. Bring him in a year or two when he's learnt not to.'

'Who was a babby once?' said Nurse, cheerful and persistent. 'All babbies smell. I'll fetch him. I'll bring the pair of them.'

She brought him, dribbling and worse. 'Master Alan,' she said. 'Just like his da and his ma, but mostly like his da. You should see him in his bath. If I didn't know better I'd say it was you all over again, which it is, of course. Quite different from his little cousin. But she is a girlie.'

'The other one is not his cousin,' said Robin. 'She is only a waif or stray, and ought to be in an orphanage.' There were always orphan cousins to be reared in castles, landless girls, unthriving youths, saying 'Yes, my eame, no my eame,' and eating good provision. But they ought to be able to prove who they are, as the meals came round.

This other baby had been found on the drawbridge one morning, and taken in by Nurse, who was determined to bring her up pretty, because you can't do that with boysies, can you?

Robin was gloomy and did not care. Nurse took both babies away and tried to make them both pretty, but couldn't stop them from scowling expertly at each other.

The leaves fell again for the second time since Robin's return. A fever from the Crusades drove him to his bed, and he lay in a darkened room. Night after night the table filled in the hall below, and the Lord of the Dale did not come to its head.

Robin came out of his bed to find that some of his delirium was true and that Nurse existed. There was nothing he could do about it. On some wakeful nights, when he could hear her mumbling to the babies next door, he wished for a roving band of paynims to capture her (or better still buy her, because then he would not be obliged to rescue her), and remove her to their own country. She would of course then take Jerusalem, and it would be lost to reality. No, there was no way of ridding himself of Nurse.

At dawn fever would return, and he would lie under its ugly charm, and wonder what the world would be like if he had designed it himself.

But he recovered in spite of Nurse's potions. He grew well, but older.

'My, aren't we building a neat little barbican,' Nurse began to say, much too often, as Robin put weight on round his waist. Castles have barbicans, an extra bit of fortress outside the main gate. Not all of them have a Nurse; only mild things like boiling pitch.

Time went by in the castle and in the village beside it. As the years went on Alan and Margaret began to understand that nowadays was nowadays, and that this was their own time. They heard old histories, but preferred new tales the world told round them. In the greenwood wolves and wild boar ran, deer tiptoed, and the bear clumped its way about. Leaves grew, and fell again.

One by one the servants and tenants, copyholders and foresters, keepers and coppicers of Eastmarch, where Meric should have been Lord, made their way to Robin.

'Our own Lord and his family are gone,' they said. 'We have no one to protect us. Eastmarch castle crumbles on its hill. Shall we ask the King for another Lord? Or will you protect us?'

Robin sent men to look for Meric. He was not to be found, on his own lands, or at court. There were tales about his not coming back from the Crusades.

'I left him not a furlong from his own door,' said Robin.

The King said, 'Time will tell,' or quaint Norman proverbs to that effect.

Time went slowly by. The King forgot Meric. The Eastmarch people began to own their houses, to fence their lands, and even to stay out late at night, singing. They could be heard through the greenwood.

'Disgraceful,' said Nurse. 'We don't want to hear such a rude dirndum, my chicklings,' she went on, covering Alan's ears and little orphan Margaret's. 'Such things shouldn't happen to babbies. There should be a way to stop them.'

At that moment, trying to cover the babies' ears and change nappies at the same time, she clumsily ran a pin first into Alan and then into Margaret. Alan bit her. Margaret turned black in the face. Under the trees the Eastmarch people yo-ho-hoed.

'Music,' said Nurse, sucking a bitten thumb. Long ago, when the orphan Margaret was found on the drawbridge, there had been a strange bendy pin holding some baby garment in place. But it had fallen in the moat before Nurse could work out whether it merely stopped the pin sticking into the baby, or worthily stopped the pin sticking into Nurse. Both babies now had their speciality, tantrum.

'Drat these pins,' said Nurse.

'Dancing,' said the Captain of the Guard, out on his battlements, hearing the Eastmarch people disturbing the peace of the greenwood. 'My Lord, shall we go out and deal with them?' He thought of joining in a reel or two, to increase the surprise, then sticking spears through the dancers.

'Go down to the village and see that my people sleep without hearing Eastmarch people,' said Robin.

Time went on going by. Alan and Margaret grew up together. Granny Shaftoe stayed in the greenwood edge, under a Great Ash Tree, with her creature pulsing in and out of visibility beside her. Once it was invisible for many months, because Sir Ailred sprinkled it with holy water when Granny Shaftoe came near a funeral in the churchyard. They pulled the priest out of the grave, where he had been tipped, and he said his Latin backwards for a year. The creature yowled for the same year, because being made good hurt it.

Nurse said, 'It's a thrill, never mind exciting,' because she thought the creature had winked at her, or fluttered an eyelid in admiration.

Years went by. Alan drew out from babyhood, toddled, walked, ran, grew tall and fair.

And as for Margaret, well, thought Nurse, pretty is not what I would call her. That's beautiful, is that little madam; and no good will come of it.

Margaret was to learn to prick her fingers with embroidery; Alan to dull his wits with Sir Ailred's Latin and simple arithmetics, often in trouble trying to add impossibles like seven and eight.

THREE

Alan Goes Fishing About Now

Alan of the Dale was acting out the siege of Jerusalem to his cousin Margaret. He had the weapon skills, though no experience.

'You weren't there,' she said, sensibly, drawing a great thread through her tapestry, and pulling it out again because it had come through the wrong hole. 'See what you have made me do. That would be very frightening if this was a real landscape.'

'My father was there,' said Alan. 'Knowing the story is like being in a real landscape.'

'He did not see Jerusalem,' said Margaret. 'There, *that* is the right place.' She did not mean Jerusalem but the tapestry.

'It was not far over the next hill,' said Alan. 'He was with Meric, the Lord of Eastmarch.'

'No one knows what became of him,' said Margaret.

'There were lions,' said Alan.

'You should be at your lessons with Sir Ailred,' said Margaret. 'Nurse is calling for you.'

'Lessons!' said Alan.

Then Robin, his father, called him to go to Sir Ailred. 'You are still a child,' he said, 'and must do Arithmetic, not Adventure; Deuteronomy, not Dragons; Legal argument, not Argonauts.'

'When I am Lord I shall have a man to do them, as you have,' said Alan.

'You must know whether the man is doing them right,' said his father. 'But tomorrow is Ascension Day, and those who know their work have holiday.'

'I shall go fishing,' said Alan. But first he had to go to his Sir Ailred's lesson.

It was about *tres (III) operarii* digging a *cisternam* in *duodecim (XII) dies*, so *quamdiu* would *novem (IX) operarii* take?

Alan said he would rather dig the cistern than do the arithmetic. Sir Ailred told him that digging holes was indeed all he was fit for, threw the book at him, and sent him home. 'Your idleness is an affront to me and an impertinence to your father,' he said. 'Now wake up and go.'

'I have been making Norwich stitch,' said Margaret, when Alan got home, showing him her embroidery. 'It

47

looks well, but I have done enough. There is too much teaching, and you are cross.'

'Oh, the book did not hit me,' said Alan. 'It never does. Tomorrow I shall fish at Saint Oswald's Well, deep in the forest, where the fish are best.'

'May I come with you?' said Margaret. 'I have never caught a fish.'

'I shall teach you,' said Alan.

'I know Saint Oswald's Well,' said his father after church the next morning. 'I caught fine fish there once, I think. But take care, take care.'

'You have told us about that,' said Alan. 'You and the lost Lord of Eastmarch.'

'Remember that the well is in the wilderness,' said his father. 'And take care.'

'I shall bring back the biggest fish there is,' said Alan.

'Bring back the biggest fish you catch, that's all,' said his father.

The path through the greenwood led past Granny Shaftoe's hut under a Great Ash Tree. Alan whispered what he knew, that one wall of the hut was the tree itself, that she lived with a cat, or dog, or monkey, maybe an imp.

'I think she's like a witch,' said Margaret, 'the way she looks at me, the way she walks at night.'

'She is a friend,' said Alan. 'She cured my wart. She

48

will tell us if we should not go.'

Granny Shaftoe was in her garden, gathering herbs. Something ran about in them, out of sight but swaying the tall agrimony and alkanet.

'Where are you going, young Alan of the Dale,' she called, 'with a pretty rod and a slender girl?'

Something looked from the garden with one eye.

'To fish Saint Oswald's Well, dear Granny Shaftoe,' said Alan.

'Saint Oswald's Well is in the wild,' said Granny Shaftoe. 'And the wild is in the Well.'

'Christian folk keep holiday today,' said Alan.

'And fishes don't?' asked Granny Shaftoe.

'She is a witch,' said Margaret.

'Speak up, young Margaret,' said Granny Shaftoe. 'Speak out.'

Margaret wished she had not said a word.

'You'll want a meaty bait,' said Granny Shaftoe, bringing from her apron pocket something pink and coiled. She threw it out to Alan's feet, where it rolled and curled as if it were still alive.

Margaret stepped back from it, and Alan closed his toes, not sure what had been thrown.

'Take it up,' said Granny Shaftoe. 'That's what's left of my wild winter pig – the tail! The squeal went first, then the fat; the puddings, then the pork; the chaps,

then the hams; the bacon, then the skin; and last of all
the stalk.'

'Is it dead?' asked Alan.

'Who knows?' said Granny Shaftoe. 'Does the tail
know when the throat's slit?'

The coiled tail had stopped writhing. Alan picked it
up. It was hairy, dry and stiff.

Granny Shaftoe's creature put its head out from the
nightshades and watched. It was hard to decide
whether it was a cat, or dog, or fitch, bawson, serpent,
or some other thing, because it continually changed its
mind about what you saw.

'Go to your fishing,' said Granny Shaftoe.

'Is it safe to go?' asked Margaret, because what was
happening seemed no good start to holiday.

'What hasn't happened might not,' said Granny
Shaftoe. 'What might happen hasn't yet. Be careful
what you catch and what you keep, for what you catch
today, that is what you must keep.'

'I shall use the bait,' said Alan. 'Come on, Margaret.
Thank you kindly, Granny Shaftoe.'

Round the next bend they were alone in the forest.

'If she were wicked,' said Alan, 'my father would
have sent her away this long time since.'

Nothing followed them under the trees; only deer
rustled in the glades, bees clustered under sweet

trees, and birds flew over them.

They came to the still clearing with Saint Oswald's Well at the far side, the water lipping and tripping, and all round greenwood quiet as midnight.

'It is peaceful,' said Margaret. 'I hear the clouds go by. The water is so clear, yet so dark. It is deeper than I can think.'

'There'll be fine fish far down,' said Alan.

'I'll help you thread the rod,' said Margaret. 'Is it not like a needle?'

'Something like,' said Alan. 'The line goes here, and here, the hook tied on like this. Do not touch, the point will pierce your finger better than it pierces the pig's tail, and then not come out.'

'Are you using that?' said Margaret. 'I do not like it very well.'

'It is an ugly bait,' said Alan, 'but Granny Shaftoe knows best. Now, here's my float — see it bobbing up and down.' He let the pig's tail sink down the water, and waited.

'Alan, this is no sport for me,' said Margaret, when she had watched for a time. 'I shall go and gather flowers of the wilderness.'

'Do not go far,' said Alan. 'Or be long away.'

'I'll come back soon,' said Margaret, 'to see your fish, and then catch mine.'

She crossed the clearing, taking a flower here and there among the grasses, going under the trees for those that grew there, reaching up into a bush for fragrant blossom, making a posy for her uncle Robin.

Alan set the pig's tail drifting down the water again, and yet again, but the fish ignored it. I must fish the deep, he thought. Something larger may live there.

He cast the pig's tail over the middle of the pool and let it sink. It went down and down, less and less distinct in the shadows, until he could see it no more, and the line slanted taut from the rod end. Nothing happened for a time.

Then there was tingling in the rod, as if a mouse nibbled the far end.

'Margaret,' Alan called. 'I have a catch.'

Margaret did not reply.

Tingling turned to trembling, as if a rat bit at the pig's tail, and Alan set his feet on the bank, ready for a long pull from a great fish.

Trembling turned to shaking, as if a calf tugged the line. Alan took the slack of the line and held.

Tugging turned to a struggling pull, as if a dog tore at the bait. The rod bowed under the weight.

The line began to lunge and plunge, as if a man hung on it, struggling to escape.

Alan hauled at every slack. He called for Margaret to help, to watch at least. She did not come.

The dark pool swirled. Something lifted in it. There was a head with teeth, a back with fins, and limbs much like claws. A creature writhed in the deepest part of the pool, where water began to boil.

Alan drew in the line bit by bit, until the catch broke the surface with great bubbles.

It rose out of the water, tall as a man, not standing, but floating with great effort.

'This is not a fish,' said Alan, letting go of line and rod, and getting to his feet in alarm. 'What is it? What have I caught?'

There was a sighing breath from the monstrous thing that was raised there, neither fish nor man. The tight line seemed to hold it up.

'Do not throw me back,' it said, not clearly, unused to speaking or breathing. It moved its limbs as if it did not know how to use them. 'Do not throw me back,' it said. 'Oh, do not, do not.'

Alan was horrified. But he overcame his fright. His instincts would not let him allow the creature on the land. He found his knife and cut the line.

'Oh do not throw me back,' said the monster; but it was too late. With the line cut it could not hold itself above the water, and it sank down again.

The surface of the water settled still again. The darkness subsided, and the shadow of the thing went down with it, until there was nothing left.

Alan was stunned by shock, and unable to move or call out. He lay beside the cut line in a swooning state all the rest of the day.

He did not see something crawl from Saint Oswald's Well, and across the clearing into the greenwood.

Margaret did not come back to him. She came back to no one. She was not there when Lord Robin came searching for them.

Sir Ailred and men of the village scoured the greenwood for her, but she was not to be found.

The Captain of the Guard brought his men at the double pace. They searched the greenwood too, left and right, finding nothing.

Alan lay many days on his bed, unable to speak of what he had seen. He knew that the monster had wanted to be caught, that both Granny Shaftoe and his father had told him to keep his catch, and he had not; and because of that Margaret was lost.

Granny Shaftoe sent a smelly ointment to rub on his chest and clear his head. Sir Ailred brought the sum about *tres operarii* to take his mind off things. He got the answer at last. It was *quattuor (IV)*.

'What is the good of that,' he said. 'When I am *unus*, and *unus* is I?'

'You mean *simplex*,' said Sir Ailred.

FOUR

Alan's Second Bidding at the Well

The harvest ended with storms. Men struggled in the fields with damp stooks of wheat. Robin, Lord of the Dale, sent household men and soldiers down to help. They grumbled in the wet, doing as much harm as good, not knowing the proper fashion, they said.

Alan had been laid in his bed in the north tower for a month. His father Robin, the old Lord, had been weakened with sorrow and distress at losing Margaret. She was not his, he said, but he had given her all he could, though she was unrelated and he had no duty. When she disappeared he felt that she had meant it, and given him no thanks for bringing her up.

'Thanks come even from strangers,' he told Nurse.

'She was a teedle-twink,' said Nurse, dabbling a tear from her nose-end. 'But you never can tell. Shall I sell her clothes, the ungrateful weasel?'

Robin asked Alan how he was.

'I have idled the summer away, Father,' said Alan. 'It is time I put my hand to something.'

'If you go to the fields, go soon,' said Robin. 'The crop is under water.'

Alan spent wet days in fields, his shoulder under bushels of grain, or against the back of a stooded cart, or pulling a horse from new boglands.

'Bitter times,' said the village folk. 'See the black spot on the grain; feel the heat in the stacks. We shall winter poorly.'

When the fields were empty, water rose in the hollows of the land, laying ponds by every house door. The castle moat brimmed full and dripped over into the cellars.

This winter there were no boars, there was no oak or beech mast for the village pigs, there was no walking in the greenwood for man or beast. The deer fled to the far mountains, and there was no meat.

Leaves dropped into slime and turned black. Murky waters rose among the trees.

Last summer, at Ascensiontide holiday Alan was calling for her, full of excitement about a fish on his line. But Margaret had her own occupation for the time being.

A fish on a hook is one thing, she thought, but a real

fawn under the leaves is much more. It wobbled its nose at her, and looked with large eyes.

'I will stroke you,' said Margaret, thinking she had charmed it. 'Do not be afraid of me.'

Far away Alan called to her, to come and see.

Margaret sent him a thought about what she was busy at. He will understand, she told herself.

The fawn's front feet twitched, and its ears heard something else, rustling in the thicket.

It will be the mother, Margaret decided. But she will let me stroke her fawn. She will love me too.

She had a picture of herself being found under the leaves, like a fawn, but in a pink silk gown, wearing a silver chain round her neck, fine as hair.

She had been found, she knew, in a basket at the castle gate by the guard coming to raise the draw-bridge, one rainy night. He thought she was a kitten and was about to throw her and the basket into the moat when the silver chain caught on his thumb, the links broke and part of it fell off.

The Lord of the Dale had been sure she was of noble birth, because of the clothes, silver chain, blue eyes, and because Nurse said the baby was an inkle pinkle twinkle, oh no, it's a girlie, look!

Was the lonely fawn's mother coming busily through the hazel bushes? Deer are timid and silent: what approached was another beast.

A voice grumbled hoarsely under the trees. Did it roar, or speak words in some rough way?

Margaret's back felt as if a cold knife had run up it, taking all power of movement from her limbs. But her eyes still saw and her ears still heard.

At that instant, her view of the world changed. The greenwood was no longer part of the home she knew, but strange and dreadful. It was not a fawn she saw, but the dinner of a wolf. She herself was food for another creature, who would leave nothing of her, not even the silver chain.

She wanted to call Alan, but her voice was locked in her throat. She gazed with a sort of horror at the fawn, until it became unreal. What she could see became curiously flattened, as if it were stitched on canvas.

The fawn, for instance, stopped having a fine silken coat of dapple, and liquid eyes with sky and Margaret herself reflected in them. There was now only a dull coarseness, with no gleam or reflection, still full of beauty, but woollen.

Some distance away was the clothy bellowing of the other creature. Margaret had an idea that it was a needle tearing its way through a tapestry picture, because she had to understand something.

The fawn got up, its edges broken by the roughness

of its new texture. It started away, and in a slow, long, moment had gone, as if it had been picked out and the background place it left darned over.

It hurried away, becoming real, Margaret was sure, as soon as it was out of sight.

She looked at her own hands, and was not ready for what she saw. They had changed. They were now impressions of themselves in colour, with no detail and no settled edges. When she put them together there was a sensation of woolliness, with stiff canvas at the back, like tapestry again. The feeling that hands should have about themselves had gone away.

The hands were difficult to take apart, because the same skin-coloured stitches made both of them, and the sensation was horrible.

She dropped stitches from her eyes, where she should have dropped tears. Her plaits were simple herringbone now – in a tasteless yellow.

Something moved in the real greenwood beyond the stitching. Not far away there was true reality, true living, and she could hear it.

But no sound came from her mouth. Her voice was caught in the loops she was now made of.

The dyes darkened all round her, and she became part of the night, some of its dusky shades, cross-stitched in common colour with a tree.

Daylight came, and as the day grew brighter she grew more separate from the background, and could move about, a very slow walking. But she was never clear of its drag. Wherever she went the hole she left had to be filled in, and until it was she could not leave. She was a long time in each place, and began to know it well.

The empty patch where the fawn had been was freshly darned, with the stitches yet to fall flat with the others, like trampled grass not yet standing straight again.

The thing beyond was still there, sometimes chuckling grimly, or giving a broken-up grainy roar.

In the space between stitches lay real greenwood, with occasionally a passing forester, a running of deer, or a sounder of boar. But the wool of the tapestry was a cage, and would not let her through.

She saw what had made the noise. It came splashing through the water on the ground, hunting, among the trees, its length supported by many legs, its head lowered and seeking scent. It was scaly and strong, and its wide mouth had great teeth. In the teeth it carried a forester, while still seeking for more.

When it did not find more it swallowed what it had. Then it lifted the great head and howled. The howl alarmed Margaret more than seeing the man being eaten. That happens to someone else; but when the monstrous creature howls your name – and she was sure of that – then are you next? Even sheltered by being stitched flat, was it possible to be safe?

Granny Shaftoe was driven from her hut by flood early in the winter. The guards would not let her in at the castle gate, thinking she had come to complain.

'I shall not speak to her,' said Lord Robin, busy with his own thoughts. 'Let the village have her.'

Granny Shaftoe would not leave, and none of the men dared touch her to carry her away. She stayed where she was. The men were unable to keep guard.

'Why?' asked Alan. 'What is she doing?'

'Standing in the rain, and no one can go past her,' said the Captain. 'She isn't taking up space, a little old skinny thing like her. It isn't that.'

'No,' said the men, 'it's what she has with her.'

'Like a cat,' said the Captain. 'Or the like.'

'Jack here says it's a ghosticle,' said a man. 'Edward says it's a megrim, and Thomas thinks it's a were-stoat, and nobody don't like it not no-how.'

'Not a proper thing of the world, that ain't,' said the Captain.

Alan felt relief at hearing about the thing; now he

was sure it existed: if solid soldiers and their Captain saw it, then it certainly did.

'You could get her away, sir,' said the Captain. 'The men are a lot of old women, if you understand.'

Alan went out of the little postern alone. The men sat round their fire, not wanting to see what happened next. The rain fell on Alan, and the planks of the drawbridge were green and slippery.

Granny Shaftoe stood on the stone end of the road that led to it. Beside her was a small dry patch among the puddles, where the creature sat. Two eyes, and a thread to connect them, hung a foot above the ground and watched all that went on.

'Now Granny,' said Alan.

Granny Shaftoe did not waste time on greetings. 'Your father told you,' she said. 'I told you, the catch itself told you: Keep what you catch, do not throw me back. You did not keep the catch.'

The creature's eyes changed from gold to purple then to black, fully open like alien flowers, staring at Alan, diffused and yet intent.

'Oh Granny,' said Alan, with surges of sadness at having to remember. 'Such a bait, and so strange a catch, so long ago, though in this very year.'

'In the same year,' said Granny Shaftoe, 'the evil continues. The catch sank down the Well, and now its waters have risen into the fields and greenwood. I have been driven from my hut, and no man has done such a thing before, Alan of the Dale.'

She lifted her hand towards him, with all her fingers pointing. The thing beside her became fully alive, a striped cat on whom no rain fell, its eyes completely hollow, showing only blackness within.

'Granny,' said Alan, 'sad times have come, but can they be my fault?'

'Sad times have begun,' said Granny Shaftoe. 'There are more to come. Often I know what may happen, and sometimes I tell what I know. The waters of the well are rising now; and I cannot bear to look. Remember, young Alan of the Dale, you did not do the wanted thing.'

The creature beside her vanished. There was the dry patch on the stone until the raindrops sprinkled and spread and hid the place away. Granny Shaftoe turned and left. Whatever walked beside her at length became the same as the splashy mist raised from the path by the rain.

'That's better, sir,' said the Captain. 'I've never known the lads so uneasy. Shall I draw them some beer?'

'No,' said Alan, because he was old enough to know about soldiers. 'They have nothing to worry about.'

The Captain sneezed a bit, because he had made promises about the beer. The men looked out into the rain and grumbled about everybody.

The winter went on wet and gusty. Even the time of snow did not freeze clean, and there was chilling clinging slush on all feet, both indoors and out.

Food came cold to the castle table, the kitchen made songs about fishes in the gutter and frogs in the butter; and the smoke blew down the chimneys.

'These are miserable times,' said the old Lord of the Dale. He had brought his sword down from the wall and was polishing it himself. 'The rust is striking in. We must keep swords bright.'

Alan polished and greased his own sword. Night after night they sat together, lonely but busy, rubbing decay from swords and armour.

One night the wind sighing at the chimney top brought another sound. Both paused in their work, because the swords in the hands responded to the far noise of some distant thing.

The Captain of the Guard came, shouting orders over his shoulder, sending men to new watches.

'What is it?' asked Robin.

'Something out in the greenwood, my Lord,' said the Captain. 'Large unidentified beast calling, not in the heraldic manuals; not on the church pew-ends; nobody has dreamed them; unless your lordship knows. Eaten a couple of the slowest men.'

The cry was all they heard. Alan and his father spent a wet night on the curtain wall, listening and watching with the men, but nothing was seen, and no more heard. Not knowing is great terror itself.

'It was something passing by,' said Robin. 'Or the wolves going into the mountains.'

The sun shone a little as the days grew longer. Leaves grew, and rain stopped. Ground dried, smoke began to go up chimneys instead of down.

Men went to the forest, but came back saying they could not reach another castle because of the flood, and that the world had forgotten them.

Granny Shaftoe came to the end of the drawbridge again. The soldiers sent for Alan at once.

'Young Alan,' said Granny Shaftoe. 'I have waded water, swum the storm. I have searched the future all winter long and come to tell you what I saw. Crossing the tide I met a wild pig swimming too. As he went I took his tail, and here it is.'

She held it up, coiled and pink like any pig's tail. The creature by her side opened and closed its eyes and purred a very little in approval.

'What this time, Granny?' said Alan.

'Do you not understand, Alan of the Dale?' said

Granny Shaftoe, shaking the pig's tail. 'Take line and hook, and fish again the same place with this bait. This time keep the catch, no matter what.'

'Shall I be safe, Granny?'

'All that is here will be safe,' said Granny Shaftoe. 'But what is not here I cannot speak about.'

'And Margaret?' said Alan. 'What of her? Is it too late?'

'All time is too late,' said Granny Shaftoe. 'It is broken before we get it.' She turned, and left.

Either side of the road through the greenwood the trees stood deep in water. There was a strange sinister beauty of sky below as well as sky above. No birds sang or flew, and even now in spring dead leaves were beginning to fall.

Where the road turned towards Eastmarch Alan took his axe to saplings and made a raft, lashing poles together, and with another he punted the raft across the open water to Saint Oswald's Well.

The waters of the Well were clear, like an eye under him. The depth was dark with distance.

He tethered the raft to a bush. He put the hook into the pig's tail, lowered the bait into the clear depths, and waited for his catch.

It wants to come, he thought, tying the line to his wrist, and it's not so large I cannot handle it; or Granny

Shaftoe would not send me.

The line grew taut, as it had before. The raft rocked on the water, and waves hurried from its sides. The catch began to shake and haul, and rise.

It came swiftly this time, from deeps to surface.

It rose beside the raft, many times larger than it had been, its teeth as long as Alan's hand, its head as broad as the raft, its eye now like a plate. It was the Worm in the Well. It towered above him, finned and winged, and spoke in sighs and rattles.

'Leave me in the water, boy,' it said, like the rolling of logs. 'Cut the line and leave me to my rest. Leave me be.'

Its head smashed the poles of the raft under Alan's feet. 'You shall not take me,' it said, under the water again, drawing Alan into the depth. Alan held hard to the line.

But with no breath in his body, and drowning, the line slipped from his wrist and he had to let it go. It was part accident, and part panic. In a moment he was above the water in the debris of the raft, and the Worm had gone down again.

But I am free, Alan thought, while he coughed and chocked, while it was more important to be alive than to be successful. Then, swimming to the road, he knew he had failed again; that he should still hold the line, and have drawn the Worm after him; because Granny Shaftoe knew, and had told him.

Overhead the clouds rolled together; below, the greenwood filled with darkness, blacker than nature.

FIVE

Alan in the Holy Land

Birds were singing like the scraping of metal on metal. The light of day was harsh and unloving, unforgiving.

Alan was lying in a hard bed in a strange room, with an aching head and sore bones.

'Did he go fishing then,' said a voice he knew well but had grown out of. 'And what did he catch?'

Alan's mouth was full of old leaves, he thought, and earthworms – something that moved about. It was his tongue trying to say something.

'Go away, Nurse,' he said, making the earthworm work at last.

'I don't even get thanked for bringing him back to life that was found drownded at the edge of the greenwood when he went fishing,' said Nurse. 'Those that brought him up from being a tiny boy should get better thanks than being told to go away, because

70

who introduced him to Sir Manners?'

'Please go, Nurse,' said Alan. 'But do not frighten the soldiers on the way out.'

Nurse liked that sort of remark, and roared with laughter. 'You're feeling better then,' she said. She went cackling down the spiral stairs.

Alan continued to feel ill, and worse, as he gradually recalled what had gone before. But he slept, and had to feel better, or Nurse would feed him soup from a spoon, and talk, and talk.

The birds outside began to sound natural. Glaring light in the room turned to sunshine. The pain in his head began to be only inside it, not the whole world knocking at it from outside. His tongue stopped decaying.

The Worm of the Well had left him in a turbulent flood among the smashed remains of the raft. He had been at the centre of a wild whirlpool, and though he swam to calmer waters beyond, the calmer waters retreated in front of him. In the end, just before he drowned, the whole greenwood had been in a gale, waves whipping under the trees and tall tides surging, branches swinging and creating wind, lightning snapping and glaring overhead, thunder rampaging in the tree tops.

It had been nightfall before calm had come again,

and so dark a night that he could not move from where he was, washed up on the old road.

He had called out in the blackness, and his voice had come back a thousand times in echo from the tree trunks; the continually moving waters had laughed back; and overhead something had fluttered its wings.

Not far off something bellowed, and more than once there was a shriek.

And still, these many days later, Alan was on his bed, no wiser than he had been, thirsty for any drink at all, and hungry without the fancy for food, stronger but still not the person he knew and slightly hated.

He lay sleepily, thinking he might wake again and be back in a better world yet. Below him the castle went on with its daily business.

He was woken by something small and heavy walking on him, treading about gently like a cat or dog. He put out a hand to push it away.

It hissed at him, spat, and hit him twice with open claws. Then it immediately began to purr and knead bread on his chest.

Alan looked at the back of his hand, where blood flowed. He kept the hand in front of his face and looked at the cat.

There was nothing to be seen. Only the weight, the

noise, and the kneading went on, without the cat. Also, the room seemed indistinct and clouded, with all its lines and angles bent out of shape.

Alan sat up cautiously. The invisible cat retreated to his legs and stopped purring. It uttered a threatening growl. It was not now quite invisible, but had become that blurred shape he knew from meeting Granny Shaftoe so often.

Granny Shaftoe herself stood by the door.

'I'll come no further, myself,' she said. 'I came through the guard unseen, through the gate unknown, up the stairs unheard, and now I see you, Alan of the Dale, who never listened when I could be seen and known and heard.'

'I see you now, Granny,' said Alan. 'I hear and know you.'

'It may be too late,' said Granny Shaftoe.

On Alan's feet the creature grew all at once heavier, and solidified into sight for a moment like a bawson, or badger. It snapped its teeth.

'Too late for what, Granny?' said Alan. 'I cannot tell what happened.'

'I can,' said Granny Shaftoe. 'Did you fare well, fighting with that fish? Did my bait catch, and did your promise keep?'

'Oh Granny,' said Alan, 'that was no fish, but some

dreadful other thing, the same again but grown greater than a man.'

'What else did you suppose?' said Granny Shaftoe. 'It has eaten creatures of the wilderness until now. If you had brought it home all might have been well, and you and your father seen your Margaret again. But you did not do the wanted thing; again you did not do the wanted thing! Worse, far worse, is yet to come, for you and those about you. There are things I dare not tell.'

The creature on the bed opened great eyes, yellow like a bear's, and something grasped at Alan's feet with paws wider than them.

'Quiet now,' said Granny Shaftoe to it. 'Well, young Alan of the Dale?'

'What shall I do, Granny?' he asked. 'What deed is there to put things right? What shall I do?'

Granny Shaftoe laughed then, and the thing on the bed grew to the mighty weight and size of a tree, the tendrils of its roots tight about his heart.

'Go seek your fortune now,' said Granny Shaftoe. 'You ought not to hear what happens next at home around us, nor think of it. Go into the wide world away from here. Go, sharpen your wits, grow strong, and after seven years come back.'

'And then?' asked Alan.

'Then?' said Granny Shaftoe. 'I cannot see so far. Often I look, as often I am afraid. Go, and return no sooner than I told you. Come, friend.'

The creature shrank down to a cat once more, allowed its eyes to glint gold and green, and followed Granny Shaftoe out of the door.

An hour later Alan himself went dizzily down the stairs, holding to the central column, slipped past the Captain of the Guard, crossed the drawbridge, and went off into the dusk, not through the village, but into the greenwood again.

'I shall not see again,' said Alan of the Dale, in the desert of Syria, a day from Jerusalem. 'I shall not live.'

He expected the paynim's sword to drop on his throat with no further delay, but nothing followed.

After all, the paynim had suddenly rushed out from behind a rock, with no warning at all, no challenge, no arrangements about the fighting about to start, in fact not a single word. But outside Jerusalem, in the desert hills, anything may happen; and when you are being squire to Sir Edward so might everything else. But nothing much was happening, in fact.

Only silence was going on, in its quiet way. In the distance one or two of those desert dogs were yelping at one another, over some scrap of bone.

Alan sat up. He had a lump like the bowl of a chalice on the side of his head, and he was dazzled blind. But his head did not fall off. No paynim sword had sliced through his neck. All he had were bruises from falling off his gallant horse. Well, his patient donkey. After all, he was still only a squire, with no sword, no wages, nothing, except maybe a tip when he left Sir Edward's service. And with Sir Edward that was not likely – Sir Edward could only be generous when he had money.

Alan opened his eyes, and the whole hot landscape dazzled and quivered round him. It was as if Granny Shaftoe's creature had come and filled all space, waxing and waning in that fashion.

But Granny Shaftoe was years behind him now, and half a world away. The present world contained Sir Edward, plainly to be seen. Sir Edward was riding off side by side with the paynim who had leapt out to attack him.

Sir Edward and the paynim were talking. They were laughing. They were occasionally slapping each other on the back, as if they were friends.

Alan's donkey was standing among the rocks considering some thorny grass. She was good at that.

Alan and Sir Edward had come up on the ridge to see what lay beyond it. Their camp was down in the valley where there was room for it. But a camp low down can be watched from above, and then attacked. So the King had sent Sir Edward up to look, and Alan had gone with him in case someone had to walk back, and to hand out weapons if they were needed.

Alan and Sir Edward had been ambling along the path when the paynim had ridden furiously towards them, shouting out his foreign battle cry and waving his paynim sword.

This paynim had done one of the extraordinary things they often did. Without arranging any of the proper details for the Conflict of Single Knights, he had charged, which was extremely impolite.

'Ruffian,' Sir Edward had said, and prepared to knock the fellow off his horse. 'I'll stitch him up with his own sinews, may he never be untied without a pitchfork.'

When the ruffian was off, Alan's job would be to sit on him until arrangements were made about a proper fight, and Sir Edward was properly accoutred.

The paynim cheated by rising out of his stirrups, standing on his saddle, swinging his sword, obviously intending to lop Sir Edward's head off quite neat and simple, meantime laughing in a way Sir Edward considered vulgar. A bit like the donkey in one of her good moods.

The laughing stopped as suddenly as it had begun.

The sword was all at once not being waved, the paynim was slowing his horse, Sir Edward was shouting.

That was when Alan fell off a donkey that had begun to walk backwards and forwards at the same time and tripped at both ends.

Now Sir Edward was riding away, as if he had met a friend. But he was riding with a paynim, so that could not be the case.

'Hoy,' shouted Alan. He had to look after his knight, and if he was a bit familiar Sir Edward would only shout back, swear a bit, and not be offended. 'Sir Edward. Ed.'

Sir Edward looked back. He spoke to the paynim, and their horses stopped. Sir Edward rode back.

'I haven't any cash,' he said. 'I'll catch up with you some day, Alan. I don't need your services any more, after what's happened. Or, I say,' he called to the paynim, 'can you lend me a bezant, or something, to pay this lad off?'

The paynim rode back to them. It appeared, after a lot of speech, he had no money either, but, Sir Edward explained, 'you could have one of his wives, take your pick, ha ha.' It was evidently a joke.

In the end the paynim gave him an old English sword, rusty, greasy, chipped, the gilt handle unravelling, but complete with a scabbard, captured from a Crusader or found somewhere. Sir Edward said, 'Thanks, old man,' to the paynim, and, 'Run back to camp, Alan.'

And then the two of them rode away, still talking and guffawing.

'Goodbye,' said Alan, and, 'Ha ha,' said the donkey.

They (Alan *primus*, and the donkey *secunda*, as Sir Ailred would have pointed out) left the mountain top and went back down to the camp.

The camp had moved. The tents were gone, the horses absent, the army itself nowhere to be seen. Of course, no one tells the squires anything, except to stop it at once if they have a moment to play fustibal.

Four nights later, leaning against the wall of the temple built by Solomon, having eaten common country bread and drunk of Jerusalem water, Alan cleaned the sword.

The Crusade was over. At exactly the same moment, a few days earlier, the paynims had decided to give up Jerusalem, and the Crusaders to go home or go off to Tyre and Sidon to play golf, the game developed from fustibal that later became cricket and rugger. The fighting was over, and there was suddenly plenty to eat, if your knight had given you real money. That was why Alan had eaten only bread and water.

It was dark before he had finished, but even so he

knew he would be disappointed. It is always so, he thought. The sword was in worse condition than he had thought at first, and no one (and he tried everyone) would consider buying it.

His cleaning dislodged a thick layer of resin, probably gum arabic, to expose tracery below the gilt handle. He could not see what it was by the twitching flames of a camp fire; but its presence meant that the owner could be traced, and his heirs could claim it back. There would be little for Alan, whose honour it would be to find the family of that Lord and give the sword back to them. It was not Alan's to keep. He slept disappointed.

Then, with the night ending, in the dawn coming from the east over Jerusalem, Alan's skin rose and prickled down his back. Those first rays showed him three linked rings across the pommel of the sword, with the boar's head above them. A devout paynim had covered the owner's sign because it displayed an abhorrent animal, the boar.

These were the arms of the Lord of Eastmarch, and this was his sword; and Alan had to take it there, Though he knew that the family was no more in its place, yet there must be a rightful owner, another next Lord of Eastmarch. It belonged to Meric, now lost to the sight of man, but still the owner.

Fully more than six years had gone by since Alan lay on his bed and spoke with Granny Shaftoe; and the seventh would be fully over by the time he had walked from Jerusalem to the Dale. And this, he knew, was what Granny Shaftoe had seen and not dared tell him. But through her wisdom life was coming together again.

I shall see my father again, he said to himself. There had been no joy in leaving without a farewell.

When the gates of Jerusalem were opened he took his way out alone, on foot, with a few coins in his pocket. He had managed to sell the donkey. The new owner was still trying to make it start. Alan left quickly, having no more with him but the knowledge of his destination; none of his destiny.

SIX

The Worm in the Greenwood

In the sickly summer of one of those years the hay lay limp on the field while new grass grew below. The sun was not strong enough to make the cut blades crisp and dry.

Herlew turned them with a many-toothed wooden rake, whistling slowly to himself, tee too, tee too, taw, taw, taw, now and then made a little remark like 'Herrumpididdle' or 'Tumble-umple-ew', depending on whether he meant 'Alas' or 'Alleluia'.

It was usually 'alas', with the hay coming to nothing, and if he got it in it would likely burn the house down, if it didn't he would starve, and these were bad times, taw, taw, taw, herrumpididdle.

But might have been worse, tumble-umple-ew.

He started another dismal windrow. A melancholy bird went 'Yoip-yoip-yoip,' and in the hedge some creature scraped and scuttered.

Herlew thought about a bag pudding, later on, full of bits of fat and stuff that stuck in your teeth to last the night. 'Tumble-umple-diddle,' he sang, the delight turning to longing: there would be no pudding and no fat and nothing between his teeth that night or for many a night past.

'And nobody doing nowt about it, generally what,' he muttered. Tee tee, too too, taw, taw, taw.

Something walked out of the greenwood, black as a pig. But the wild pigs had gone and the tame pigs been eaten. Granny Shaftoe was under the trees.

'You should be gone, Herlew,' she called.

'Maybe, Granny,' said Herlew. 'But I ain't.'

'If you go you'll live to regret it, Herlew,' said Granny Shaftoe. 'If you stay you won't.'

'Herrumpididdle,' said Herlew, at what she said first, and then, 'tumble-umple-ew.'

Granny Shaftoe stepped away under the trees, out of sight. A thing with a tail followed her.

The sun politely went behind a cloud – what was to happen ought not to be watched. Something scraped heavily in the hedge beyond Herlew, breathed mightily in the field beside him, stamped the ground behind him, and scurried in the hay his far side.

It had more legs than a cow. Herlew had not done

arithmetic at school, because there was no school, or much arithmetic in those days. But there were more legs than two cows, or three cows, or four, or five. That was more cows than there were in the world, he knew. And since this was not a cow, or cows, then it didn't matter.

But it did, because he had come to the head, which had eyes like buckets of water, teeth like churchwarden's staves, a tongue forked like a cart shaft. All Herlew had was a small wooden rake with a handful (five) of teeth missing and no tongue whatever.

His own teeth were loose now, shaking in their sockets.

The Worm from the Well looked at him in a slightly hopeful way – a touch of tumble-umple-ew, perhaps – as if it might be glad. It breathed in roughly and pitiably, and its great tongue moved.

'Look at me,' it said, unnecessarily – Herlew could not look anywhere else at the moment.

Herlew's chattering teeth bit his own tongue and tears came into his eyes.

'I know the feeling,' said the Worm, kindly. Too kindly, Herlew thought; it's going to ask me for an extra day's work.

'I have a question for you,' said the Worm. 'Will you take my daughter to be your wedded wife?'

'Is that all?' said Herlew, bravely. 'No.'

He saw a growing look of herrumpididdle on the creature's face, and fell down in a faint on the damp hay. As the thing ate him he began to understand what Granny Shaftoe had said: it is essential to be alive in order to regret. Then it was dark inside, tee tee, too too, taw, taw . . .

'They do not listen,' said Granny Shaftoe, down under the crooked oaks of the forest. 'He should perhaps have said yes, but I cannot know the answer. There are years to go, yet.'

The hay resolved the next day into silage for three hours by the church clock, then rotted gently back to compost by the calendar.

The cobbler had his mouth full of brads. One by one his tongue brought them to the front and pushed them out head first, used to the sharpness and the taste. He went on with his work silently, as far as anyone else could tell. Except of course for the hammer tap-tapping on the boot in front of him as the sole was laid in. On the bench a single candle-flame shrugged its shoulders at each hammer hit. Leathery dust sparkled in its light and in its smoke.

But inside himself the cobbler was full of music, just as a boot is full of foot, tap-tapping to his hammer rhythm, all the toes of his mind jigging on the lining of his fancy. Instruments so far unknown to man played their harmonies and tunes, and great chords and arpeggios flooded his understanding.

'Why can't they hear it?' he would say to himself. 'It's in there, why can't it get out?'

Tip tip tip tap, went the hammer; and boom boom boom tara went the fanfares of the mind. The thick leather of boots turned to the thin resounding vellum of drums; the tacks in his mouth drew the strings tighter; the threads of stitching were looped into violin bows; and the concert hall of his skull resounded with great pieces of art.

He kept the pieces next to his soul. Each had a feeling and a name. If you asked for Ladies' Court Shoe, size seven, narrow fitting, grey suede, the song was very different from the tune for Gents' Oxford, black, twelves, or the rhapsody of Explorers' Brogue, brown, waterproof, full sizes only.

Today was a pair of boots, regulation size, for the Captain of the Guard up at the castle, and the tacks were going in left, right, left, right, in marching order, and the tramping tune was going up hill and down dale with the legions.

While the cobbler and his thoughts are far away and out of sight, the candle flame that glitters has begun to show a fright. For the marching of the feet he hears is not only in his mind; there is something close behind him that is of another kind.

It speaks, like the deepest note of a fifteen-foot drum, through teeth like the bars of a window. 'Cobbler,' it says.

Every note falls from the cobbler's mind. Half his pins spit themselves on the floor, half go into his throat, and some he has forgotten about from an earlier job bristle through his cheeks from inside like a brass beard.

'You want boots or shoes?' he asks, looking along its length and calculating how many feet and dividing by two for how many pairs of footwear. 'I can do a reduction for quantity. I don't mean they are a size smaller but the right size and they don't cost so much and . . .' It never does to be afraid of customers, but some things do not like being talked to, you can tell.

'Shut up,' said the Worm. 'Don't talk with your mouth full. Will you marry with my daughter, and have her as your wedded wife?'

'If she has as many legs as you I couldn't keep her in shoes,' said the cobbler. 'Sorry.'

It's best to be firm, he thought. But the tongue in his mouth felt like the tongue of a boot, and the roof of his mouth like hobnails, and his throat like the sole of a clog.

'Sure?' said the Worm.

'Sure, thanks,' said the cobbler.

The Worm put out a tongue like a tarpaulin and pulled him in. 'You taste terrible,' said the Worm.

'Don't talk with your mouth full,' said the cobbler, thinking of music more and more abstract until he was digested.

All night long the Worm spat out tacks and hiccuped semiquavers.

'I should have had my boots resoled before last night,' said Granny Shaftoe, limping up the village street, 'because it is sometimes too late to mend.'

She shook her head. The thing beside her shook its head and shimmered in the candlelight from the empty cobbler's shop.

The Worm belched a complete symphony, and crawled away among the trees in a fugue, feeling baroque and counting its legs to see whether any of them were its last ones.

The traveller came slowly into the village on a sunny morning. His name was Gorburt, and he travelled slowly because he was extremely short-sighted – he had to wait until the ground came into focus before putting his foot on the next bit, and the problem had grown worse as he grew taller.

When he was a baby lying on the floor of the hut, he had watched his mother walking about with her head in the clouds. He thought it was normal. As he grew older she grew a head, so he could recognize her from a great distance of about five feet.

For a year or two he could see his own feet, and where he was walking. Then he had grown too tall for that, which was awkward now that he travelled about. Not being able to see far, he had seen close. He had learnt to write and sharpen a pen, and become a wandering scribe. He could write a letter for you, or even a poem.

He knew he was in a village, because the constable had taken money from him, and children were throwing stones. Stones were town weather he understood, and the children always stayed more than six feet away.

One came too close, and he caught it. He got bitten, but he held on. 'Where am I?' he asked.

'Dale,' squealed the child. Gorburt thought this was some form of swearing, and shook it a bit.

'Don't cuss me,' he said. 'Where am I?'

'Dale,' screamed the child. 'Name of the place, mister. This is the High Street, that's the castle, and let me go or Granny Shaftoe will get you.'

'She won't bother,' said Granny Shaftoe, passing by.

She had had stones from time to time. 'But I daresay the Worm will get you, my lad.'

'Dale?' said Gorburt. 'Is it a pretty place?'

'Gerroff,' said the child, biting again. Gorburt let him go.

'There's nothing for you here,' said Granny Shaftoe. Her creature jumped on a wall, walked in front of Gorburt, and became invisible before his eyes.

'What's that?' he said. 'First it was ginger, or black, and then it's not there or invisible without going away, and . . .' But he stopped. Something extraordinary was happening to him. What was only invisibility to some eyes was a vastly different thing to his. Most people saw disturbed air through the creature, or found that everything beyond had become fuzzy. It was the opposite with Gorburt. His eyes were pulled into focus when he looked through the cat. For the first time in his life he could see more than six feet.

He did not see much – a tree far away, a road leading to it, distant mountains, cloudy sky, and a long shambling animal approaching the village. The cat became opaque again, and walked out of sight.

'That moggie has funny dreams,' said Gorburt.

'So do I,' said Granny Shaftoe. 'What are you doing here?'

'No trade so far,' said Gorburt. 'But I haven't got sat

down yet. I'm a scribe, and I'll write a letter for anyone, if they'll pay.'

'Not many folk left here,' said Granny Shaftoe. 'They've gone, or been taken. And not many visitors either. Did you learn reading, too?'

'Heard of it,' said Gorburt. 'It's tricky stuff, Great A, little bouncing b, and that. Then when you've eaten the words they're still there: disgusting, if you think about it; and a lot of funny flavours. Have you ever tasted "marcescent" or "festoon" or "quell"?'

'I never learnt to read,' said Granny Shaftoe, 'so I don't know what they say. Can you tell me?'

'Do you want a poem?' asked Gorburt.

'Yes,' said Granny Shaftoe, thinking about it, not having had one for years now, hoping he meant marshmallow.

'Let me settle down in this corner,' said Gorburt. 'Poems cost two pennies.'

Granny Shaftoe waited. Her creature settled in the middle of the road and stopped all the traffic. The horse pulling the traffic quietly went to sleep, used to being terrified.

Gorburt laid his writing desk on his knee, sucked his pen, had a good big black spit, dipped the pen in it, and was ready. He wrote,

Early in the cabbage
One important Thursday week,
They hurried in and got it done,
And that was very that.

'Shall I go on?' he asked. 'I think that's the bit where they did it.'

'Did what?' asked Granny Shaftoe.

'I don't know,' said Gorburt. 'They didn't teach me to read my own writing. This is my poem and I know how to write it.'

By now the creature had got up from the middle of the road, miaowed like a calf, and jumped on Granny Shaftoe's shoulder to whisper in her ear.

'I have to go now,' said Granny Shaftoe. 'I've just had a vision of the future and I want you to enjoy it as you deserve. Goodbye, and good luck.'

'Thank you, thank you,' said Gorburt, to the space where she had been. He was used to people vanishing as they spoke.

He saw that he was surrounded by legs. It was not unusual for crowds to gather to watch a man writing a poem. He was pleased. For two pennies a time he would copy it out as often as necessary. When a crowd of feet revolved about him, he glowed with pride. This was not so small a village, after all. 'Two pennies a poem,' he said. 'I'll write it down.'

'A question first,' said someone invisible, with a great cavernous voice that had swallowed boulders.

'Of course,' said Gorburt.

'Look at me,' said the questioner.

'I'm a bit short-sighted, Sir,' said Gorburt, blinking about him. 'My goodness, what a big dog you have. Has he any good tricks?'

'I ask the questions,' said the voice. 'Will you marry with my daughter and take her as your wedded wife?'

'Why not?' said Gorburt. 'You keep the dog, and I'll have her. Is that a bargain, then?'

'Of course not,' said the voice. And the Worm ate Gorburt, while he shouted to it to call its dog off.

'What dog?' said the Worm, with an inky black belch. 'I'll have it for afters.'

The village idiot, or gob-drool, had never had it so good. Along come thic nice friendly beast and do talk to he. No stones, no kicks, not even laughing at I. How bist thee? he do seem to say, and did open its mouth, and inside did be a lovely comfy pink tongue, just like a lord or lady do sleep on. Gob-drool do climb in, see, with thiccy-there-thang great thing to hold to, like teeths to help I up, and I do curl up on the pink tongue like a bed, put a thumby in my mouthy, and it do slide

I right along back down in under through, squeeze, lovely, squeeze, down the long lane in the dark, lovely. Bed do squeeze I to sleep and I be spaced out utterly.

Gob-drool do climb out and have that over again, never had no feeling like that afore. Gob-drool be going to bide here for ever, don't want nothing else. Nobody done that to I since I did cut my teeth. Then, old tongue do spit I out in the road, mouth do close, just like a door, no good knocking, won't open. And legses do trample on I head to tail. Ugly old Worm, hope you do swallow bad dreams and nightmares. And who got a wet tongue, anyway?

The Worm could be heard gargling below the bridge, coughing out morbid fancies.

SEVEN

The Worm in the Village

'Amen until the next time,' said the priest, Sir Ailred. 'I'd say more, but where are my people?'

There was no answer. People were not in church. The Worm lurked round the village day after day, and it was a scuttling sort of life everybody led, to get from house to house, or to the pond for water; no one dared till a field, and the cows could not be fetched in because they had been eaten one by one.

The little church was the last safe place, and Sir Ailred stayed in it. But now there were no congregations, no funerals, and no collections.

'Is the Worm one of God's creatures it's worth asking the bishop about?' said the priest. 'If I met it would I be brave? Would I be missed, and if not shall I tell the bishop now? And what would I say to it – the Worm, not the bishop?'

'Amen,' said a voice, and a great many people seemed to run into the church together and stand there out of breath and breathing heavily, in and out together, like one person. Or thing.

If I don't look round, said Sir Ailred to himself, it will go away. I'll go on saying my prayer, *Nunc dimittis* and so on.

But all he could think about was bread-and-butter pudding, which he did not like. He thought about it because he now felt rather sick. It's the withered currants, he thought. Or the septic custard, and the awful heaving noise of the spoon lifting slabs of it out. I had it twice a week when I was a child, three times at Oxford, four times at theological college, and every day but Sunday now. It's the story of my life.

'Amen,' said the voice again, in a snappy sort of way. 'Have you finished, Sir Priest?'

'Or the story of my death,' said Sir Ailred.

The Worm took a turn round the font, and a procession up the centre aisle, where its tail twanged the bell-ropes and shook the bells, making the melancholy jingle used for calling out the fire brigade. Its head was at the chancel steps.

'Take a pew,' said Sir Ailred. 'Several if necessary. What can I do for you?' He was astonished to find that he could speak at all, but forty years of bread-and-butter pudding are preparation for the real trials of life. 'There's nothing wrong, I trust?'

'It's about my daughter,' said the Worm. 'She's causing me some anxiety, and I'd like to see her settled.'

'What can I do?' said Sir Ailred.

'Can you take her to be your lawful wedded wife? Will you marry with her?'

'To have and to hold from this day forth for ever more?' said Sir Ailred. 'My congregation would feel outnumbered, for one thing, and . . .'

'So you won't?' said the Worm.

'And the bishop wouldn't approve of monsters in the vicarage.'

'It's not the time for funny answers,' said the Worm.

'It was a funny question,' said Sir Ailred. 'I'm best at the ones about if *decem (X) ambulatores* take *quattuor (IV) dies* to travel from an *oppidum* to an *urbs, quamdiu* would *quinque (V) ambulatores* take?' But the Worm's mouth was opening, and there seemed to be more teeth than there had been Kings of Judah, in the region of *quinquaginta quinque (LV)*, at least.

'Stop,' said Sir Ailred. 'I am actually a bread-and-butter pudding. You will not like . . .'

A moment later the Worm belched and the roof fell in. It climbed out of the ruin and grew another pair of proto-legs, like a caterpillar. It went off into the greenwood to think about withered currants and septic custard.

Granny Shaftoe heard the church bells tumble down and came to look.

'Hungry in the greatest degree possible,' said Granny Shaftoe, seeing the Worm's footprints in the dust, 'to be thin enough to enter the church.'

In the greenwood the Worm howled.

'Let us hope it is just indigestion,' said Granny Shaftoe. 'I shall speak to the Lord of the Dale. Of myself I see no future, and never did, so I cannot tell. I shall regret speaking to the Lord of the Dale, but all the same I must do it. Come, Thalumar, leave a mouse for the morrow.'

She went to stand against the castle door, until they let her in and she spoke alone with the Lord of the Dale. Then she went home, and waited.

Robin, Lord of the Dale, came to the greenwood the next day. The years had made him no younger, but he felt he would still offer a bonny fight to anything that would stand against him. His sword was ready, as it always was, and his armour bright.

He stood under a great oak tree and shouted out a challenge.

'Where is the monster Worm? Come out and show yourself. I have come to finish you. This is to be the last act of my life or of yours, or even of both. I do not care.'

The Worm came prickling through the trees, marking and scoring them as it came, marching like an army, circling the Lord of the Dale where he stood, and coming face to face with him.

'I shall ask the questions,' it said, rather like a furnace. 'So be prepared.'

Granny Shaftoe, at the greenwood edge with the remaining villagers, hoped the answer would be right, but knew it must be wrong. Thalumar nestled in her arms, and they were both full of dread.

'This time you must be satisfied with my answers, master Worm,' said Robin, dropping down his vizor, ready for any teeth or any claws.

'Will you take my daughter for your wife, my only daughter, your only wife? Yes or no.' The words came out like flames, hot and rising.

Robin shouted in his helmet, so that words came bent and muffled from the corners of it, out of sequence, but defiant. 'I answer not with words but with a sword, take this, take that, Worm.'

The Worm snarled. It did not waste time. It advanced with open mouth. Robin cut off an ear, and enraged the creature. He prodded the sword up its nose and made it sneeze. He aimed a swipe at its tail, which was not looking what it was doing.

'Amen,' said the tail.

'Shut up,' said the Worm.

The tail made amends by getting behind Robin. Robin put his back against the tree to prevent his being surrounded, and settled for a long fight.

'None of your formal set-piece battles,' said the Worm. 'I've got a life to lead too, you know.'

'Not much longer,' said Robin, getting both hands on the sword hilt and aiming for the tongue.

'I knew that when I couldn't see it happening,' said Granny Shaftoe, 'that it was bound to.'

It did. The Worm closed its teeth on the sword, rushed round the tree one more time, brought its head round again, and nibbled Robin up, spitting out larger pieces of armour and cracking the rest.

The sword dropped from its lips, it spent a moment disentangling itself from the trees, and trotted easily off into the greenwood, uttering new but gentlemanly burps.

Granny Shaftoe picked up the broken sword and took it to throw into the moat.

'Two more years before young Alan may return,' she said. 'Shall we live so long?'

EIGHT

Margaret in the Greenwood

Nurse watched the village from the narrow window of her turret room. In between long stares at the few houses and huts with roofs on them she was sorting out her collection of lace.

'Peasants die out,' she was saying to herself. 'Only the better class of people live on irregardless.' She said it out loud, because no one else listened to her.

And it couldn't possibly get in here, she thought, looking at the window itself. Only the wind gets through that.

Some way off in the greenwood the Worm had some sort of noisy hiccup, from a combination of bread-and-butter pudding and pieces of armour.

Nurse sorted her lace out into another order. There were only two orders, because there were only two pieces of lace, but that made decision all the more important. It was taking years to decide.

If he kills it, she thought, then the villagers will keep on multiplying, and that will be the end of us better folk. I mean, these days I'm as good as one of the family.

Actually, though, the old Lord doesn't think of me like that. 'Nurse this' and 'Nurse that' and 'hand me a cushion, Nurse' and 'those children should be in their beds' and 'there will be no need for you to return to the table, Nurse' – that's what it's been all these years.

But young Alan. Ah, that's bound to be different. I've been like a mother to him. Yes, I have.

She put the Chantilly lace to the left of the Brussels lace and considered the effect. A brilliant thought came to her mind, and went away before she could catch it. But it was still in the room. For the time being the Chantilly lace stayed on the left.

What happens if I forget which is which? she thought. The collection will become worthless. I wish I could read and write and put labels on them all. It was quite fun when the Worm ate that scribe. It spat in the moat next day and all the drinking water was totally black for a week.

Her thoughts wandered back to her proud position in the household.

It was me that told his father it was a boy, because I was there and I saw him first. 'Alan shall be his name,' he said, 'Alan of the Dale he shall be,' and his poor mother smiled at him and went to sleep for ever, poor dear, I'm sure we would have got on wonderfully and a few more kiddies would have brightened the place up. Like a mother to that one I was, him and his lordly little ways, 'Nurse this' and 'Nurse that' and 'hand me a cushion, Nurse' and 'I should be in my bed' and 'there will be no need for you to return to the table, Nurse', until there wasn't a more devoted slave than me. But that makes me more like family, humble as I am.

Each one gone, she thought, glancing at the village again, makes me one higher up. Soon there'll just be us. Me.

She tried the Chantilly lace to the right of the Brussels lace. These decisions made her head throb. The thought came back and bruised her meditations. It lurked nearby in a threatening way.

I'm glad I haven't got three pieces. I'd be into the big time then, and have an artistic director. And admission charges. But peasants would see the collection, and that couldn't be right.

The Worm made a roaring noise again.

'It's dying,' said Nurse. She was sorry about it. She

would have left it alive until there were no peasants left, only aristocracy, including herself.

He'll be back soon, she realized. I hope he doesn't bother to bring its head back. That dragon he killed, way back in '83, '84, long before Alan was born, didn't half smell after a couple of weeks. Why do things keep when they are alive and not when they are dead?

Her thoughts returned to Alan as a young child. More than a mother, I was. Nurses are trained, but mothers think its natural. But instinct doesn't tell you how to change a nappy; it's training, or you don't know where the pins will end up.

I wonder where he ended up, she continued, her thoughts drifting in their usual way. It can't be my fault. But bad times have come to us all.

At the far side of the moat Granny Shaftoe was shuffling along the road, carrying bits of something long. She lifted the long bits above her head, and threw them into the moat. There was a fierce shout from the Captain of the Guard. Granny Shaftoe turned away towards the river and the greenwood and the Great Ash Tree where her hut once again was.

Nasty old woman, thought Nurse, straightening the Brussels lace once more. Just at that moment the stray brilliant thought came to her again, and she sat transfixed by it, staring at the table, as it unfolded in her mind. Or exploded softly.

An utterly tiresome thought had pushed its way into her head, a way of making pins so that there was a springy coil at one end and a little narrow hood at the other, and you pushed the point of the pin into the hood and called the whole thing a safety pin, and it would not stick into the baby or Nurse. How generous of me, she decided, to think about the babbies too. Then she thought of the drawbacks, which were that no one would want that sort of pin, and if they did, there was no way of making it, or even several, without engaging in Trade, which was common. She pushed the tedious idea away and concentrated on the lace again. As ladies do, she was sure.

Her head ached now. She put the whole collection back in its box and went out of the room, down the spiral stairway, to the inner courtyard.

Down there no one took any notice of her. The Captain of the Guard was organizing his men, without any warning, into doing something quite unusual. They were about to drain the moat.

'But there's always warning,' cried Nurse.

'You can't do it just like that,' shouted the cook.

'Ducks need water,' complained the duck-keeper.

'Emergency,' said the Captain of the Guard, briefly.

'Any trouble and you'll be court-martialled and pegged out for the Worm.'

'I'm family,' said Nurse.

'You're litter,' said the Captain. 'Away lads, get turning on that windlass.'

The windlass would lift the gates and put the water into the river Dale again, but why that should be done was not clear.

'We'll let you know,' said the Captain of the Guard. 'I'm in charge.'

'His Lordship is in charge,' said Nurse, dancing about round the Captain and round his men. The men were heaving at the windlass, but the wooden gates were sticking in their slides.

'Ha one, ha two, ha three,' shouted the Captain. 'Put your backs into it, lads.'

The gates stayed tight. Then there was a reluctant creak, and part of an inch of movement at the windlass. That represented ten times the movement at the gates, but it was a start.

'His lordship shall be informed,' said Nurse.

'There will be an enquiry,' said the cook.

'The ducks will come off worst,' said the duck-keeper. 'You'll upset them beyond all calculation.'

'Go away,' said the Captain. 'I warn you.'

'I shall not,' said Nurse. 'You are not in charge of

me. I should be in charge of—'

She did not finish her sentence immediately. The gates shifted suddenly and the waters of the moat gushed out in a great spout, sinking down to reveal the dark mud that centuries of household sewage and stagnation had produced. The mud bubbled and stank, and quite a lot of it writhed about because muddy creatures lived in it.

The twelve spokes of the windlass lost all their resistance. They spun without any hindrance, and bowled the twelve men over, so they went somersaulting across the yard like portions of an exploding star, striking whatever was in their way.

One of them cannoned off Nurse, driving her towards the balk cushion of the rear curtain wall; another came off a turret and caught her on the rebound, and a third nudged her nicely into place for a full-on shot from a fourth. She went into the centre side pocket of the main doorway of the castle at an angle, rolled through it with much back spin, hit a stanchion on the side of the drawbridge, rose into the air, came undone, so to speak, floundered in the air, and dropped into the black depth of the exposed moat bottom. Where she floundered still further, and excited eels clambered up her sleeves, for which no training had equipped her.

'—you,' she said, finishing her sentence. Or perhaps beginning one.

'Get yourselves picked up lads,' said the Captain. 'You aren't hurt, and if you are you'll grow another one. Get down in the moat and find the object.'

'I'm here,' called Nurse, sitting up, astonished to find the moat had been so deep and that she was in a huge ditch.

'That's a mud fairy,' said the Captain. 'Just find his Lordship's sword. We'll bury that. That's all that's left.'

'What do you mean?' called Nurse, 'all that's left.'

'His Lordship perished fighting that here Worm,' said the Captain. 'Hence and therefore why I am in charge under martial law until the successor or heir to the Lordship returns, young Alan of the Dale, now absent on his own business.'

Then one of the men found what they were looking for, the muddy and bloody sword that Granny Shaftoe had dropped into the water.

'Right, get it clean, shining, sparkling, and laid in the coffin as soon as possible,' said the Captain. 'General rules of war, if no remains, then bury combatant's sword; if no sword bury armour; if no armour bury anything obtainable. I remember once we buried a tin of baked beans a young gentleman had been a-opening in his tent at the battle of Sporran and which was the only trace to be found after the natives had done with him.'

The soldiers lined up, knee-deep with mud, and stamped across the drawbridge into the courtyard. The gates were lowered, and the moat began to fill again.

Nurse climbed slowly out of it. At the castle side of it the bank grew steeper towards the top. She had difficulty in getting up the last ten feet, and no one came to help her.

Then, as she reached up to the edge of the drawbridge, her other hand discovered something small and metallic under the ooze. 'It feels like my old glasses,' she said, and clung on to the thing.

She heaved herself up on to the bridge like a toad, and sat hunched on the edge for quite a long time. She tried to look at what she had picked up, but there was too much mud. And when she had stood up and walked in there was no water to be had. She shook eels from her elbows, and in exchange the cook let her stand by the great kitchen fire until the mud dried. Then he obligingly cracked her open with a steak-mallet.

She was able to examine the thing next morning, when light came again. Each end of it had a fine silver chain hanging from it, and both these ends were broken. The chain matched the one found on the baby girl long ago. 'But Alan was my first and best baby,' said Nurse. 'The little girl was an inkle pinkle twinkle, but you have to be kind to an orphan laid at the castle door dressed in fine clothes.'

The piece she had found must have fallen away from the basket the baby girl had been in. It gave an immediate clue to the baby's family, being the three linked rings of Eastmarch.

'Well, well,' said Nurse, 'there's glory for you, me nursing all these noble children. Fancy. And we always did wonder what became of Eastmarch, because there's little enough there now, they tell me.'

She stowed the ornament or charm away and sat down to think of important things like the lace collection and its attendant problems. Like a true aristocrat, dismissing further thought of the safety pin as unworthy, while thinking that would be a good name for it.

It was becoming clearer to Margaret that she could see beyond the stitches whether she wanted to or not. And the other side could see through to her.

At first it did not matter. A bird had been startled by a mere opening and closing of her eye.

A fox, turning leaves under the trees had stared when she tried to part the blotches of colour, or stitches, that hemmed her in. She had almost formed a hole of simple clarity with two fingers, but that had turned the fox away.

A black and white bawson had been less shy, and had approached her when she tried to attract it. Those teeth, she thought, could rip away the false canvas that held her captive. But it had gone too.

The long creature that ate men had appeared again, and turned her heart chill by looking steadily in her direction, even when she had not moved or, for that matter, really looked.

It had looked and looked, however, and then gone away. Its muffled roar had come back to her time after time.

The next time it was contemplating her from a much shorter distance. She could hear its tongue move. Luckily the night had come then and made her indistinguishable from the background.

There was no escape from it. She could not move faster than sewing, she found. Each hand movement meant the unpickings under the fingers, each arm shift like becoming unglued; to move a leg was like removing skin – all painless, but slow as growth.

One day the background blinked at her. She had

been looking into the eye of the creature, close against the place where she was. It gazed, and blinked again.

The creature glistened, inches away, and sniffed. Near her feet its nostrils sniffed. Its eye looked level at hers. She heard it try to speak.

She waited for teeth to burst through the fabric like needles and take her, as it had taken a forester. But it did not do that. Instead, a tear formed in each eye, ran down its huge roundness, clear and blue, and soaked into the stitches as a spreading dampness.

There was a sob from the throat of the beast, and the eye went away. It turned and walked off under the trees, its bearing dejected, its many legs rambling idly, sad sobs rumbling in its throat.

It was not about to eat me, thought Margaret. It did not mean that. It wants some other thing.

Then it was night again, and its distant voice was far off indeed, echoing under the mountains.

It has not bellowed at me, she remembered. It has only looked.

The next day the place where the tear fell was not like the rest of her close surroundings. The dampness had begun to turn to the minute brightness of reality. Where there had been the impression of leaves there were now the veins and skin of actual leaves. Where there had been the fill-in stitches between leaves there was now true space. When her hand went down there, after hours of being dragged, her fingers became solid with true detail again, and could move as they once did.

NINE

Alan Speaks with Granny Shaftoe Again

The Worm came to weep against Margaret on other occasions. She could see it clearly through the worn place it had made with its first tear.

In some ways it was a joy to her to see things as they really were; but since the Worm would certainly eat her when it had made her real enough, there was something alarming about the matter too.

But day by day it took away the thing that imprisoned her. Until one day, after it had gone, she found that she could slide out of the coarse dappling of stitches, and was free beyond them, herself again, fingers and limbs complete, clear, and unattached.

She did not know where she was. In some ways, only a moment ago she had been gathering flowers for Alan while he fished; and he had called to her

while she looked at something under the trees.

There was a gap in what she knew, and nothing to put in it. She could find nothing to show where she had come from, which way to go. All round lay the quiet greenwood, some of its floor lying empty in clear acres, some of it tangled with the spread of bushes, some of it stocked with bracken and boulders.

Of the place she had crawled through there was no sign. She was without a landmark. And still dressed, but without a stitch on.

She called for Alan, and her voice was eaten up by space, absorbed by leaves, wasted on the ground. There was no reply. A bird lofted into the air with a crackling of wings.

Further away the Worm lifted its voice in reply, perhaps; or maybe only in hunger.

Margaret stayed lost. She had no hunger now, because she was not in time, or even in known space. There is a place for Lost, and the only way out into time and place is called Found.

She was not found. Except by the Worm. It came, and she thought it was hunting her. But it acted as it had when she first began to see it, standing away and watching, and only coming closer gradually. There is, after all, a sort of time inside the place that is outside time, and things happen in it.

The creature was so shy she was sure it did not intend to eat her. It came as close as she let it, and stopped when she thought it was near enough.

It spoke to her, but she did not understand. What it now said was jumbled and muddled, scrambled and shuffled.

Margaret began to think. What was this creature? She had little to guide her, because she had not seen what had been in the Well. Might it be Alan, turned like this after drinking from a poisoned spring? But you do not depend on what people look like, more on how you understand them. This animal was not Alan. It was a bit soppy, crying and so on, when Alan would have jumped about and boasted.

'I know it is a person,' said Margaret. 'But what person? I have been frightened by it, but it does not want to frighten me. It is not the Lord of the Dale. It is not Granny Shaftoe. It is not that silly Nurse. Who else can it be?'

The answer came slowly to her.

Wandering in places completely strange, she came on a hillock in the woods, with young trees growing in it, birch and elder and ash springing up with slower oaks.

This hillock had a building on it. She picked her way up to it and found the whole hill made of the fallen walls and broken stones of a large building. The building at the top was a small tower, with roof and window and tumbly doorway.

Carved on the stone transom of the window were the three interlocked circles and boar's head of the Lordship of Eastmarch, and at once she remembered all about it, and knew this was the fallen castle of the Lord of Eastmarch who vanished in his own country, long ago. Her own lifetime ago.

Two facts came together then, that she was her own lifetime old, and that the Lord of Eastmarch had been gone just so long, both him and all his kind.

At that time a baby girl had been laid at the door of the Lord of the Dale, in fine clothes. No more was known about her.

'But I am that girl,' said Margaret. 'I know about me, and I understand my kind. I am here in the lost woodland, and perhaps my father is here too, and has stood in this tower, and carved his sign on this stone.'

It was difficult to have the next thought.

There was another being lost in this place with her, and perhaps he had been lost even longer.

But would he eat foresters? Would he hunt men down and devour them? How else, though, would you behave if you were a Worm, and that was your nature?

She left the lonely tower, and hid in the greenwood once more.

In a day or two it found her again, snaking among the trees, immensely long, swinging its head, slowing when it saw her, approaching like a cat – friendly but cautious, aware of its claws.

Margaret stood against a tree, wanting its strength against her back when she asked the question.

The Worm stayed slyly or shyly a little distance away. It gazed at her with its huge eyes. It was so big it could use only one at a time.

'Come closer,' said Margaret, and brought it nearer, and then nearer again, until it was as close as a stranger could approach. But she knew the question to ask it.

'Are you my father?' she asked.

The Worm all at once dropped its whole length on the ground, laid its jaws on the turf, and closed its eyes. Under its lids great tears swelled the skin and burst out and gushed out at the lower edge.

It sneezed. It opened its eyes. It spoke, but nothing of any use.

It rolled over on its back, greatly clumsy, and gave a great snuffly roar, a giant but pathetic sound.

Margaret ran to it and knelt beside it, and tried to take the huge head into her lap, knowing that what she had thought was true, and no longer afraid for herself.

But it was difficult to think about its way of eating people.

TEN

The Third Bidding

They had been shaking their heads for the last fifty miles and telling Alan to go no further north.

'There's no one left,' they told him in town after town, village after village. 'You might call this the end of the road.'

One day, coming to a rather primitive river without any hope of a bridge, he felt that he had come to the River Dale, and that the Dale itself lay along it on either side.

He turned left there, and followed up the bank, leaving the road that led north.

A few yards up the lane beside the water, it was as if he had come through a door that closed behind him. There was no noise on the road he had left, because there was no one there when he left it, no one talking, no one laughing, no one jingling harness. It had been quiet.

Now there was something greater than quiet, a dreary hush on the countryside. Even the grass looked round before it rustled shyly.

The horse put its ears back and walked on tiptoe, which was silly. Alan found that he was sitting in a particularly silent way, anxious not to creak or rattle. That was equally silly, because he had not been doing either.

But there was something stoppy in the atmosphere, something that made him move delicately, that said it was the sensible thing to do.

A great careless petal dropped clanging from a wild rose. All the other flowers seemed to turn and glare.

The river slid by hurriedly and smooth, without a ripple. Trees moved leaves daintily, turning them without a sound. In their branches squirrels padded furtively. Sheep whispered guiltily to one another, heads together. The sky overhead had muffled clouds across it, insulating the Dale from the clamour of heaven.

Across the muted Dale, from far away, came a roaring cry, where something had dared lift its head and announce itself.

The river shivered; squirrels seemed turned to wood; sheep stood open-mouthed; clouds darkened.

Alan's horse stopped. Alan understood what went on

in the creature's mind, because it went on in his. They had been summoned to a meal: if they answered the meal was them.

'You are all cowards,' said Alan. 'Something is wrong here, and I have a very good idea what it is, and that I shall have to deal with it.'

His spoken words shocked the landscape. A squirrel scolded him in a drastic manner. A sheep looked about to see that it was safe, and stamped a foot at him. The river decided to run underground for the next few days. It still feels safer there.

All the real wild roses turned white to this day, as we know.

'I don't care what you think,' said Alan. 'It's high time I was back. What can my father be thinking of to let the place become so miserable?'

As soon as he asked the question he knew his father must be dead, or gone on another Crusade. In either case Alan was now Lord of the Dale, and even more bound to put matters right.

'We'll do it properly,' he said. 'This is my land, and I order it to become noisy like real countryside. The wind must blow, and the river rage; the sheep must shout and the meadows rave; wild beasts must run, and the clouds must rive; men must ride and children riot.'

The Dale took a great deal of persuading. It had

begun to go back to a wary wildness, when to be noticeable was to be eatable.

'Come now,' said Alan, 'we have to be our real selves.' At night he built a huge fire, and sat by it playing a lute and singing loud and scornful songs.

By day he travelled up the Dale. Folk would come fearfully out of farmhouses and ask him to move on, because they did not want something they called the Worm to visit them again. They had run out of spare old people, they said, and in any case the Worm had become fussy, sending back perfectly edible uncles and guaranteed fresh aunts.

'The Worm?' said Alan. 'Then it is the same.'

He came round a bend in the lane, and suddenly and clearly saw the Dale he knew laid out ahead of him, with the square castle in the distance, and the village below it. The greenwood glowed all round in sunlight, and only the tops of the hills were bare.

He felt a surge of joy at seeing the place he knew, and then a touch of doubtful sorrow when he looked more closely.

There was something wrong at the castle. No flag flew. Ivy grew up the walls, which is not allowed in fortifications. The drawbridge was hanging in mid-air. The towers had stonework missing, and the curtain wall had a crack in it.

It was nightfall before he came to the village. He walked about in it amazed. No house he knew was standing. The church had been pulled open. The roadways themselves had begun to disappear because no one walked them.

The damaged castle was deserted. Alan called across the moat.

At last a ragged man came to the other side of the moat.

'Nothing for you,' called the man. 'Bridge won't work, and a good job too. We can't stand another attack. So be off, and stop your racket.'

'Nothing here, your honour,' said a ragged woman from the ruins of the cottages. 'We've all been eaten, every mannikin and girlikin of us, except the likes of me, and I'd go, truly I would, but I can't run fast and when the time comes I can't help it. And I've lost my collection and my boysiewoisey, and my inkle pinkle winkle.'

'This is me, Alan, Nurse,' said Alan knowing at once who she was. 'I know you, and you haven't changed a bit. And you've said an unpolite word without knowing, you're so old-fashioned.' But he was extremely glad, without wanting to be, to find her, because those you know are a part of you, delightful or not.

'Oh, my young master,' said Nurse, falling on her knees in the stony roadway, 'ouch, how I'm glad to see you, those soldiers turned me out of the castle after your poor father . . . well, after your father, and there couldn't be a braver man, after he . . .' And Nurse-tears, which are quite easy to come by but were quite sincere too, fell from the end of her nose and off her chin.

'The Worm?' said Alan. 'If I had done the right thing in the first place, this would not have happened.'

'It would have been something worse,' sobbed Nurse, looking on the bright side.

Alan saw someone much more sensible. Granny Shaftoe came out of the ruined village. Beside her walked whatever walked, drifting in and out of actuality like some evanescent hyaena.

'I am going to have one of my headaches,' said Nurse. 'That person's pet gives me raging allergy.'

'Alan of the Dale,' said Granny Shaftoe, conversationally, as if no time had gone by since he left, 'you will come to my hut and wait for the Worm there. That much I know clearly. For the rest, I know what you should do, but not whether you do it. If you do it then certain things follow; if not, other things will take place. I see them both.'

'I shall do what I should do,' said Alan. 'Tell me how it has been here.'

'As it was to be,' said Granny Shaftoe. 'You know the Old Lord is gone in battle with the Worm; the castle is ruined and bolted up since it too was attacked. Most of the villagers have been eaten. And there is no sign of your Margaret. What do you bring?'

'My Lord's sword of Eastmarch,' said Alan. 'I found it in the desert places of Syria.'

'Indeed,' said Granny Shaftoe. 'Come to my house. I shall lure the Worm to it, and you shall fight it. Promise now to do as the Worm begs you.'

'I do,' said Alan. 'I have failed before, but I am wiser now.'

'Are you?' said Granny Shaftoe, not impressed.

Her house was where it had been, in the greenwood, under a Great Ash Tree.

'Here you must keep vigil,' said Granny Shaftoe. 'You must be ready to fight; and in the fight you must obey the Worm. Your disobedience has brought us to this state. Now you must put all right.'

She left Alan by himself, and went out into the twilight alone. She took with her a curled pinkish thing from the brine of her bacon vat. It was a pig's tail, a bait Alan knew well.

The creature sat in the doorway and was a sentry. If

Alan stayed at the other end of the hut it grew small like a kitten. If he approached it it grew larger, more wolf than wolf, more wild than wild.

Granny Shaftoe went about her work in silence. Something out under the trees ran and trampled bushes. Something growled.

Granny Shaftoe's creature moved to one side and Granny Shaftoe came in.

'I have brought it close,' she said. 'It knows you and the bait are here. Answer the question that he asks as I shall tell you.'

She closed the door. Alan felt trapped, but thought that Granny knew best. She could hardly know less than he did.

Something rubbed against the hut.

Her cat fluffed all its fur out suddenly.

Something snuffled at a corner. Granny's candle fluttered.

Looking at Alan, peering into the room from the window, was the largest eye Alan had ever seen. Looking hard, looking firm, looking straight.

Margaret found it difficult that a Worm she thought was her father had a habit of eating people. The Worm had a problem or two as well.

'You should learn to undo them,' said Margaret,

when she had found the problem. And she dropped a tear for the previous owner of some iron greaves – the leg piece of armour – wedged between the teeth at the right hand side of the upper jaw.

The Worm rolled over on its back again, and Margaret tugged at the metal. 'It will be much easier if I put my foot on the roof of your mouth,' she said. 'It might be horrid for you, and much worse for me. Can I trust you?'

The Worm opened its mouth very wide.

'I mean, are you actually my father?' she asked, her foot raised ready to step in. Her mind was saying something about not walking into the mouth of something you would try to wake from after seeing because it must be a nightmare.

'You might have got a taste for people of any sort,' she said. 'I might be all there is in the world for supper.'

The huge tongue tried to lick her hand, which meant she fell over because a tongue your own size has difficulty selecting the hand.

'You could eat me without my help,' she said. 'All I can say is that you'd better not try with my help. I'd be a sorry supper.'

The Worm gave a sort of submissive yelp, and laid its jaws open for her. She put her foot in, and it did not bite her leg off. The piece of armour had to be worked at for a long time before it came free. She wished it did not rattle when she had it out, but of course the bones were still inside.

The Worm licked its jaw for a long time, and seemed happier.

'Or perhaps I just think you are him,' said Margaret. 'Now what shall we do? I'm getting tired of being out here in the greenwood. First it was blotchy, and now it is boring, and I ought to be getting back to Alan. He's fishing, you see, but I can't find the place.

The Worm went with her when she looked. Or perhaps it just went with her. They did not find Saint Oswald's Well, but they came across the mound of stones that had been Eastmarch castle.

Here the Worm rather frighteningly hunted up and down the heap, sniffing and scrabbling, and trying to get in at something. Margaret did not know what was there, and wished that nothing was; but the Worm seemed to think something it could eat was in there.

The Worm at last found the carving on the lintel of the tower. It had difficulty in getting it clearly in sight, but did so at last. It gave a long, melancholy howl, abandoned the search immediately, and went away. It ran off with a particular cry that Margaret had heard before, in the distance. It was the hunting howl, she supposed.

She was alone. When night came she felt safe, and curled up under a tree. The Worm was out there eating people, but that was its character.

She woke up surrounded by resting legs, the Worm coiled round her, its head resting on several of its segments, looking in at her.

When it too woke up it acted like a good parent and taught her how to stalk her prey. They practised on a tree stump, the Worm tracing a swinging track to it, swaying from side to side, uttering little growls and whimpers, then rushing forward with wide open mouth. Its mouth could bite the stump. Margaret felt very ineffective with her tiny gape, running up to a tree and threatening it with her human molars.

'I could catch something small,' she said, remembering the fawn. But she was still outside the times of her body and did not need to eat.

More often they spent time running about the greenwood romping. Margaret screamed with laughter when the Worm learnt to run backwards and forwards at the same time in a horseshoe shape. She fell down with joy when the two running halves forgot about a tree they were both passing, and became hooked on it. The whole Worm, however, sulked. Margaret recovered from her laughing, and had sore sides herself. She rubbed the Worm's tummy as well as she could, and it felt better for the kindness.

One day it said her name. She had not told it, so it must have a reason for knowing. That proved it was her father, she was sure, because what other Worm would know her name?

Then instead of running alongside, in danger of being trampled by a wave of legs, she one day climbed up on its neck, and rode.

Now they could go anywhere. But the Worm would not take her hunting. She would wake alone to hear the hunting call coming from far away.

She began to feel more alive, and often had a sense of being hungry. It had been strange to know about hunger and not feel it – better than feeling hunger and being unable to do anything about it.

There began to be a sort of disturbance in the air. Round about, in the greenwood, things were going differently. Wild flowers began to spring again; birds filled the leaves with chatter and song. Foxes and bawsons made their way along paths unknown to men; the wild boar trod his own ways on his own errands. Something was waking the land up.

One night the Worm rested uneasily, waking and walking, yawning and prowling, unable to settle. It sniffed the air, listened to the wind, then nudged Margaret awake and lifted her on to its back. She crawled along many segments to the neck, where she sat and arranged flowers gathered during the day.

The Worm went on its flowing way through the greenwood, knowing where to go, knowing what drew it to a little hut, under a big tree.

The Worm laid its eye against the window of the hut and looked in. Margaret slipped off its neck and stood beside the Great Ash Tree, slowly remembering Granny Shaftoe's hut and knowing it held unhappy memories for her. What you know is part of you, whether it delights or not.

ELEVEN

The Last Bidding

Granny Shaftoe watched. 'Do I like it, Thalumar?' she asked her creature. It rubbed its back against her hand. Under the silken fur was the lithe skeleton of cat; or under the rough coat the power of wolf; or below the spines the venom of the dragon; or maybe, as it arched its back she felt the force of eternity. But Thalumar did not answer.

'At the centre of everything,' said Granny Shaftoe, under the tree, 'I know nothing after all.'

The Worm had drawn back from the hut when Alan went out, his sword half drawn.

'Do it then, do it,' said Granny Shaftoe.

'Aye,' said Alan, knowing he had to fight.

The Worm circled the Great Ash Tree uneasily, on bare ground where nothing grew. Its head swayed from side to side.

When it spoke its voice was thick with years of forgetting how to utter, like a tall clock on Saturday before the weights are pulled up again.

'Will you fight?' it asked, and shook its head sharply, as if it had said the wrong thing.

'Say no,' said Granny Shaftoe.

'But,' said Alan, 'I came to—'

Thalumar growled. 'Say no,' said Granny Shaftoe.

'No,' said Alan, sulkily. It was like having to confess to Nurse some small sin (such as, 'Who bit the bicky? I know whose toosipegs fit that bitey.'). 'I shall not fight.'

'Will you run?' asked the Worm, shaking its head as if some small thing irritated it.

'No,' said Alan, because that must be right.

The Worm howled.

'Well spoken,' said Granny Shaftoe.

'What's left, Granny?' said Alan.

'Next time say yes,' said Granny Shaftoe. 'That's all I know; and how I know I cannot tell.'

There was a crackling hiss from Thalumar. His eyes gave light in the dusk.

From village and castle the remaining people began to gather warily under the trees, in shadowed undergrowth, only faces showing, then being hidden as they let leaves part and close.

There was a silence. The Worm did nothing but stare at Alan. Its restless feet stilled to immobility, and its swaying head became stationary.

Someone brought the light of fire from the village and spread it among the people. The irregular flame made the Worm harder to see.

Alan was aware that something more than the Worm moved under the tree. The Worm was keeping still, but some other thing urged it to move.

He almost heard a voice – perhaps some memory echoing in his ears.

Now the Worm certainly moved. It unwound itself from the tree and came towards Alan, opening its mouth and showing many teeth, roaring softly but with only a half-hearted threat. Now and then as it came it looked back to the tree, and then advanced again, more slowly each time.

'Say yes to the sorry thing's question,' said Granny Shaftoe.

A voice called out, 'She's a bad and naughty lady, Alan my duck, and take no notice of her.'

It was Nurse. Alan ignored her. Alan knew she was wrong, because she always had been and some things do not change. And Granny Shaftoe had been right so far.

'Come on, Worm,' he said. 'What next?'

The Worm hesitated. All its legs wavered, as if it were about to faint.

'Will you marry with my daughter?' it asked, suddenly straightening its legs, raising its voice to a snarl, and clashing its teeth.

'Yes,' said Granny Shaftoe urgently.

There was a shriek from Nurse, a hoarse cry from the Captain of the Guard. Alan did not heed them.

'Yes,' he said, the Worm's mouth open and towering over him, feeling foolish at being in that position and reckless at making a promise he might regret.

The Worm stopped, in some sort of astonishment, while it worked out the result of the reply.

'I hope I like her, Granny,' said Alan, able to do nothing for the moment, and hardly able to think of anything to say.

'You don't get a chance to know,' said the Worm, making up its mind, shrugging off something that seemed to be pulling at its ear. All at once it was completely throat and teeth, closing over Alan, and over Granny Shaftoe as well. Thalumar spluttered and went out of existence entirely. All Alan's sight and sound of the world was soaked into a damp set of gums, teeth, and caverns of gullet.

'I think I told you wrong, young Alan of the Dale,'

said Granny Shaftoe. 'Both of us are gone by now.'

At that speech the tongue, which had been ready to sweep Alan and Granny Shaftoe up, recoiled. Teeth and throat retreated without taking them. The gullet was hidden when the jaws closed. Alan and Granny Shaftoe stood where they had been. Thalumar sparkled with rage but sat firm – only its tail switched resolutely, as if counting down to, er, catastrophe.

There was a sigh from the watchers. Thalumar opened one eye.

The Worm retreated, then hunched itself forward again. It dropped its head to the ground, its body heaped behind it, and lay there in a submissive way.

'Alan of the Dale,' it said, in an extinguished sort of voice. 'Will you do my bidding this time, the third? You have not heeded me before.'

'It's a trick,' shouted the Captain of the Guard.

Nurse had a loud and vulgar faint.

'Say yes,' said Granny Shaftoe. 'Say yes, and this time do the needed thing. Do it.'

'Yes,' said Alan. 'I will do it.'

'My daughter will tell you,' said the Worm. 'Margaret, come out of the wilderness and stand beside me. Tell Alan of the Dale what he must do.'

Margaret was there. From her own point of view she had been there all the time, standing beside the Worm's head. Now that he spoke clearly she understood its difficulties. All it had said and could mean before had been words about eating people.

But that was only until the right time, place, and man, appeared.

Margaret had known Alan when she saw him, and wanted to run forward to say she was safe, and would he take her home? Even the prospect of Nurse had not intimidated her. She had been stopped because the Worm had had to go through its set of phrases and ideas, only hesitating when she had told it that Alan stood there.

It was when the whole phrase, 'Alan of the Dale', had been spoken, that the Worm had laid its head down and asked the final question.

As for Alan, he felt that the seven and more years since he fished Saint Oswald's Well had looped themselves round to make a separate part of life, and that now, where the thread crossed, he was able to begin again. It seemed to him obvious and right that he should promise to marry Margaret, though he did not understand how she was here and what she had to do with the Worm. The words 'my daughter' must be only a polite way of putting things. Perhaps the Worm only thought she was its daughter? Because it could not truly be so.

But it was truly Margaret, coming forward with a bunch of flowers in her arms, not smiling particularly, but unaware that time had passed since she left him.

'Why are you here?' she asked, carrying on from the last time she had been with him. 'I said I would come back with the flowers I picked for you.'

There was a commotion in the crowd of watchers. The Captain of the Guard shouted and struggled to hold someone back, but failed. Someone came hurtling across the rooty ground, tumbling and puffing and shouting about inkles and pinkles and twinkles, and reaching into some inner hidden pocket for something.

'See what I found,' shrieked Nurse, fetching up at the muzzle of the Worm, and at last getting the thing out from under her petticoats. 'Look what I found, and I had it put together, because I'd know my little girlikin anywhere, which is more than some would say. As if I didn't know.'

She reached up to the startled Margaret and hung something round her neck.

The Worm drew in a breath and blew it out again in a gale. Nurse's ample skirts were over its nose by now, and held the great breath. Nurse flew into the air and sailed across the clearing.

'Do my bidding,' said the Worm to Alan.

Thalumar watched the orbit of Nurse, then stepped

aside and caught her as she dropped towards the ground. To do this he had to take the shape of a demon with horns, talons, a tail, and sulphurous sweat, and the sort of smile that makes leaves fall off trees, turns milk green, and reduces grown hedgehogs to tears. Nurse opened her eyes, saw who it was, and fainted with joy.

'Come back, Thalumar,' said Granny Shaftoe.

'Her's my inksy pinksy,' said Thalumar, in demon English. 'I wants she.'

Margaret looked at the thing hung round her neck without surprise. She was sure, already, that she had come from Eastmarch. Now she had other things to think about.

'This creature is my father,' she said. 'Some magic of the Wilderness turned him to this shape and sort. Before misfortune came entirely on him he took me by night to the castle of the Dale and left me there. Since then he has lived in the Wilderness alone, until he found me again. Twice you caught him, Alan, which was your fate; and twice you did not do the wanted thing, which was your doom and his. But now he finds you, and you find him, and there is one more thing to ask.'

'One thing more,' said the Worm. 'One thing more to do.'

'I will, I will,' said Alan. 'Be sure of that.'

'This time do it,' said Granny Shaftoe. 'Obey.'

'Do as my father asks,' said Margaret.

'What is it?' asked Alan. All eyes were on him now; the whole world waited for his obedience. He felt that he had lost all the battle there was, and was having to pay whatever penalty the winner demanded. It was most likely to be some long quest in far places, he knew, having read about such matters. And really he wanted only to be at home in the Dale, and then to share that life with Margaret. Those things seemed obvious to him. But he could tell they were not to be. 'Tell me,' he said. 'What have I to do?'

The Worm spoke. 'With your sword cut off my head. Kill me. Kill me surely; kill me dead.'

'But,' said Alan, 'that is not the right thing to ask. I cannot kill the father of my Margaret, and then bring her happiness in marrying her. How can such a thing be?'

'Do it,' said Granny Shaftoe. 'Now.'

Thalumar dropped Nurse in a spiny thicket and came back to Granny Shaftoe's side. 'Do it now,' she repeated.

'Now,' breathed Thalumar.

Nurse groaned, ready to faint again if her handsome devil would come back to her.

'Do it,' said Margaret. Like Granny Shaftoe she

understood the importance of doing what was asked; and more than that, she knew that cutting off its head was the right thing for the Worm, and at the same time the right thing for her father. 'I am sure,' she said.

'Do it,' said the Worm, and stretched out its neck.

Alan looked round. His instincts were for killing the Worm and against killing Margaret's father. Also, he did not like the way everybody watched him, including the Worm itself.

He pulled his sword out and got both hands on the hilt. This was the Eastmarch sword, sharp as frost after months of care and polishing, filing and whetting, strong as winter, blue as night. But was its purpose to kill its own owner, something that had a human daughter? A human daughter that Alan proposed to marry, whatever her ancestry, human or not? After all, genetic modification can go either way. He hefted the weight, and looked at the Worm's neck.

It was extremely thick, and covered in scales that looked like metal. How could this thing have a daughter of any kind, human or not?

The watching villagers and soldiers held their breath, ready to be carefully on the winning side.

Alan laid the sword on the scaly creature, just to show it where to strike, to gauge the stroke, and gathered strength. He lifted it, like a golfer getting ready. He shifted his feet a little to get a better stance. He felt ridiculous for thinking of golf, but he had often seen the Scottish knights in their kilts teeing off on the golf links at Tyre or Sidon, with a little Saracen boy carrying their clubs, swords, haggis and whisky.

'Excuse me,' said the Worm, lifting its head and turning it to Alan. 'Just a moment.' And it had a look at the sword. 'Interesting,' it said. 'Not what I expected.'

'It's sharp,' said Alan.

'Yes, yes,' said the Worm. 'I know.' And it laid its head down again. 'It'll make a clean cut. Better that way.'

Margaret came to stand by the Worm's head. She reached up and pulled down the lids of its eyes. 'Just pretend you're going to sleep,' she said. She laid the flowers on its brow, and sobbed a quiet sob.

A giant drop ran from under the Worm's eyelid.

Alan raised the sword, arched his back inwards, pushed with his feet to drive his strength and weight into the blow, and swung the heavy sword down.

The meat of the Worm was insubstantial stuff, and the blade struck through on that stroke. The balance of the head tipped it forward, and it rolled over and lay still, detached from the rest of the creature.

Its eyes remained closed, but the great mouth, while remaining closed, seemed to smile. Margaret flung herself on it and sobbed in a righteous sorrow. The flowers fell underfoot.

The head died, Alan saw. But the body writhed. He turned to face the noises and dangers coming from it, holding the sword ready again.

The noises were laughter and surprise, and the movement was in no way sinister. The segments of the body were falling away from each other and each resolving into the man, woman, child, or beast that the Worm had devoured.

First of all of them was Meric, Lord of Eastmarch, who was unknown to Alan, but known to Robin, the Lord of the Dale, who came out from a distant segment and greeted his old companion.

Margaret, understanding what had happened, abandoned her sorrow and came to greet the father she had never known. Round her neck was the completed necklace with the interlocking rings.

'This is father, Alan,' said Margaret. 'You have not hurt him. Only the Worm is dead.'

'This is my Margaret too,' said the old Lord of the Dale. 'I see we shall keep her here, Meric; but that you will be not far away. Alan, you do not know Meric, but he and I fought before Jerusalem, or would have done if there had been battle.'

'We went hunting instead,' said Meric. 'And my

fortune changed. But Alan has put all things right. Between us, Robin, you have my daughter, and I have your son, and all is right.'

'Perfect,' said Nurse, swooning again in the glittering black arms of her demon.

'And my time is done,' said Granny Shaftoe. 'I'll be a wise woman now, since I lose my familiar Thalumar.'

By the turn of the year the shield of Dale was quartered with that of Eastmarch, and, borne on an inescutcheon, or little shield shape in the middle, the three golden pigs' tails.

In the Wilderness Saint Oswald's Well ran clear and safe, and men are building Eastmarch once again. Thalumar set up as smith, and Nurse as the mother of imps. They became rich by manufacturing safety pins for all the noble children, especially the long brood of Alan of the Dale and his Margaret.

Once again in the fields Herlew could be heard saying, as necessary, 'Herrumpididdle,' or 'Tumble-umple-ew,' tee tee, too too, taw, taw, taw.

The cobbler set up a factory with musical hammers, and all the shoes and boots made there squeaked in harmony, which was a marvel.

Gorburt forgot his letter and his poem, and the Worm's digestive system bleached his ink white.

Because of his short sight they made him a judge, where none of it mattered.

Sir Ailred the priest came back, repentant about causing the Worm so much pain by being indigestibly full of bread-and-butter pudding, and was made bishop. He now has cake pudding with cream, and sleeps like a cat.

The gob-drool spent several nights sleeping on the pink tongue of the Worm, waiting to be swallowed so sweetly. But the Worm's dead head would not oblige. The gob-drool had to push himself through the gullet head first, and caught his heels on the tonsils. He could be there yet: no one has been to look.

Many years later the head was taken to the British Museum of Natural History in South Kensington, where it lies in a remote cellar haunted by shrieks of artificial delight.

At the wedding Granny Shaftoe was the first to dance and the last to stop, which was where she came in.

EARTHFASTS

William Mayne

It started with a noise reverberating in the hill. David and Keith see a boy appear from the ground, carrying a candle and beating a drum. A boy from another time who will have an irreversible effect on both their lives.

Extraordinary things start to happen. Standing stones move. Giants stalk the hills. Wild boar rampage through the town.

Then David vanishes. And Keith must search through time for his friend.

CRADLEFASTS

William Mayne

David avoids talk of the past. Memories of the loss of his mother and baby sister are too painful to share, even with Keith, his best friend.

Then Clare appears, a girl the same age as his sister would have been. She knows his name and says he's her brother. David wants to believe her story but Keith is unconvinced.

Is Clare telling the truth? Can the baby girl have survived after all?

The compelling sequel to Earthfasts.

CANDLEFASTS

William Mayne

'*Something stronger than a dream was with him, something lurking and moving beyond the stones.*'

Long ago a drummer boy from another time had turned David's life upside down.

Years later, he thinks all that is over. David has a new life full of opportunity, and only his outrageous younger sister Lyddy to cope with. But the Jingle Stones still call him back into the past and into the future. And David finds he has more mysteries to solve. There's magic everywhere he turns . . .

The climax to the Earthfasts, Cradlefasts *sequence.*

SILVERWING

Kenneth Oppel

Shade, a young Silverwing bat, is the runt of his colony. When they start the long and dangerous migration to Hibernaculum, millions of wingbeats to the south, he is determined to prove himself. But he is bolder than he is strong. He strays from his mother and a storm tears him away. Then he is on his own.

He knows he must rejoin his colony in the south and so begins an epic journey – from the pigeon stronghold in the city's spires to the rat kingdom in the caverns of the ground.

Who can he trust and where will his journey end?

'. . . fast paced, cliff-hanging action . . . Recommend this one' – *School Library Journal*